A KISS IN TANGIER

Flying to Tangier to look after five-year-old Tommy is more complicated than Eve had expected: Dean, a widower, is an indifferent father, and his Arab housekeeper sinister. Puzzled and uneasy, Eve turns to Evan, a young man who assisted her before. However, when Nadia arrives Eve realises that her new-found love is doomed, although she is too entangled in the web of intrigue to leave. And when danger threatens, her only thought is to help the man she loves.

R. PR. *   PLU

Please return / renew by date shown.
You can renew at: x   FL
norlink.norfolk.gov.uk
or by telephone: 0844 800 8006
Please have your library card & PIN ready.

In   PN   P

⑯

DENISE CONWAY

A KISS IN
TANGIER

Complete and Unabridged

LINFORD
Leicester

First published in Great Britain in 1974 by
Robert Hale & Company
London

First Linford Edition
published 2008
by arrangement with
Robert Hale Limited
London

British Library CIP Data

Conway, Denise
  A kiss in Tangier.—Large print ed.—
Linford romance library
  1. Tangier (Morocco)—Fiction
  2. Love stories
  3. Large type books
  I. Title
  823.9'14 [F]

  ISBN 978-1-84782-336-6

Published by
F. A. Thorpe (Publishing)
Anstey, Leicestershire

Set by Words & Graphics Ltd.
Anstey, Leicestershire
Printed and bound in Great Britain by
T. J. International Ltd., Padstow, Cornwall

This book is printed on acid-free paper

1

Tangier! It's incredible, Eve thought as she listened to the whine of the aircraft. I'm really going to see Morocco's city of mystery and intrigue. I wonder if it is as wicked as they say . . .

The air-line hostess noticed Eve's smile and moved towards her. There was something about the attractive dark-haired girl which made her want to speak to her. Perhaps it was the wide, green eyes set in a fringe of thick dark lashes or maybe it was the novel expression of excitement and wonder on the oval face which appealed to her. Whatever it was, the hostess was unable to resist the chance of talking to her. Seat belts had been unfastened some time ago and there were a few minutes to spare.

'Quite comfortable?' she asked, leaning towards the girl and smiling at the small boy who was sitting next to her.

Eve smiled back. 'Yes, fine, thank you.'

'Is this your first flight?'

'Yes.' Eve laughed ruefully. 'Does it show that much?'

'A little. The other passengers look bored. You appear to be enjoying the experience.'

'I am now. I was scared at first.'

'Most people are, although some would deny it. I usually have the collywobbles before we are airborne.'

The girl's green eyes widened in astonishment. 'That's difficult to believe. You look so confident.'

The hostess chuckled. 'I've lost count of the flights I've made, but it's always the same. It doesn't last, thank goodness!'

Eve glanced at the small boy. 'Tommy thinks I'm a coward. He's loved every minute of it.'

'I can see that.' The air-line hostess stepped back. 'I shall have to get back to my duties. If you need anything, don't mind asking.'

Eve nodded, then put her head back and closed her eyes. In two hours and a half they would be touching down at Tangier air-port. There would be a twenty-five-minute drive in the coach and then they would be in the city. To think that a week ago I had nothing to look forward to except my vacation in a month's time, she thought dreamingly. August can be so hot and uncomfortable in London. And I couldn't afford to go away this year. She had let herself drift back, seeing again the small flat which she shared with her sister and brother-in-law; an arrangement made hastily after the girls' parents had died within a few months of each other.

Amy's marriage had been breaking up for some time and it had been painful as well as embarrassing for Eve to watch. She had kept away from the flat whenever she could, realising that any interference from her would only serve to make matters worse. Bill and Amy had to sort it out for themselves.

But it had made Eve unhappy and she had longed for the chance to get away. Then quite suddenly out of the blue the opportunity had arisen and she had grasped at it eagerly.

One afternoon when she had seen the last child collected from her nursery class, she went to find Tommy, a five-year-old boy who was in the next grade. He finished half an hour later than she did and those few minutes gave her the chance to tidy the classroom before she left. Tommy lived in the same street as she did, and as there was no one to take him home, she liked to see that he arrived home safely. The High Street in Kensington was a dangerous road for a small boy to cross unaccompanied, and it was no trouble for her to look after him. He was a quaint little boy and she had soon found that she enjoyed his company.

Tommy's mother had died when he was two years old and he had been left in the care of his mother's sister. But because Mrs Thomas had recently returned to work there had been no one to take him to and from school. Meeting Mrs Thomas one morning as she was rushing to get Tommy to school before she caught her bus, Eve had introduced herself and offered to take the boy. His aunt had been grateful and delighted and a warm friendship had sprung up between them. It was to Tommy's home that Eve found herself gravitating those evenings when the atmosphere in the flat was too uncomfortable to bear.

On that particular afternoon Eve found Tommy in a very excited mood. Usually he was rather quiet, so it surprised her when he chatted incessantly about things she could not make head nor tail of.

'There's heaps and heaps of sand, all gold!' he exclaimed, skipping with glee. 'And palm trees and umbrellas in the sun.'

'Umbrellas?' Eve smiled indulgently as she glanced down at his tousled fair head. 'You don't need umbrellas in the sun.'

'You do in Mocco, where my Daddy lives.'

She looked at him curiously. He had never mentioned his father before. 'Have you ever seen your Daddy?' she asked.

'I 'fink' so.' His blue eyes were puzzled. 'It was long, long ago.'

'Can you remember what he looks like?'

He nodded his head solemnly. 'He's wery bwown and he's ten feet tall.'

Eve laughed. 'No one is that tall!'

'My Daddy is! He's taller than anyone.'

'I expect he seemed tall to you,' Eve smiled faintly. 'Would you know him if he walked up to you now?' Too late she wished she had not asked that question. Tommy's face had puckered up and he looked ready for a few tears.

'Never mind,' she said briskly. 'You will see him one day.'

'That's what I keep telling you!' His voice squeaked reproachfully. 'I am going to see him . . . in a jet plane.

Auntie told me so this morning.' He glanced up, his blue eyes shining. 'A jet goes faster than anything.'

'I'm sure it does.' Eve was beginning to believe him. Perhaps Mrs Thomas had heard from his father.

Tommy's aunt met them at the door of her ground-floor flat. This was unusual, for normally she did not get in until thirty minutes or so later. Eve would stay with Tommy until she arrived home.

'Come in, Eve! Tea is ready for you.' Anita Thomas smiled as she allowed them to pass in front of her into the hall. 'It's quite an occasion. I've bought a cake and cut bread and butter.'

Eve smiled as she was shown the table in the dining-room laid out charmingly with a lace cloth and flowers in the centre. 'It looks as if Tommy has been telling the truth,' she commented. 'You have heard from his father.'

'Yes, I have.' Anita's thin face sobered. 'I do hear from him occasionally, but Dean never writes more than a few lines as a rule. But yesterday I had a long typewritten letter from him. That's why I left work early. I wanted to talk to you.'

'To me?' Eve stared at her in a puzzled fashion.

'Yes. I'm hoping you will help me, but I'm not certain you are going to approve.' Her eyes fell on Tommy, who was studying her face solemnly. 'Tommy, find something to amuse yourself with! Eve and I are going to make the tea. We won't be long.'

When they reached the kitchen she shut the door behind them. 'I didn't want to discuss this in front of the boy,' Anita said seriously as she dropped tea bags into the teapot and poured boiling water over them. She gave the liquid a quick stir and then left it to draw. 'After all this time Dean has decided he wants to have Tommy with him. He's asked me to send the boy out to Tangier.'

'Tangier! That's a long way,' Eve exclaimed.

'Yes. I feel rather annoyed at the

8

casual way Dean does things. When his wife died he didn't want to know about the boy. He said that he couldn't cope with a child and that his work came first. I loved my sister dearly and offered to care for Tommy for as long as necessary. I've loved him as if he were my own and now I'm expected to give him up.'

'Perhaps Dean just wants to see him; have him for a vacation.'

'I don't think so. The way his letter went it seems final. He says that it is time he got to know his son. After a few weeks he would find a suitable school for him. Dean doesn't intend to come over here. He can't afford the time. He's an American, but he's spent most of his adult life in Europe and North Africa.'

'He may be planning to return to America.'

Anita nodded her blonde head. 'Yes, that's what I think. I can't refuse. Tommy is his son. But I'm very worried. That's why I'm going to ask a big favour of you. I want you to go with Tommy and find out if Dean's arrangements are satisfactory.'

'Me!' Eve gasped. 'You want me to go to Tangier?'

Anita gave her a pleading look. 'I know it's a lot to ask. Actually Dean suggested that I send someone with Tommy. A capable woman, he said, one who could cope with a small boy and be willing to stay two or three months until Tommy has settled down. He's made a generous offer. He will pay a good salary and he's sent the air tickets.'

Eve was looking dazed. 'He's very sure that you will let Tommy go! When? I mean, how long have I got to make up my mind?'

'A week? Will that give you enough time?'

'Yes. I suppose so.' Eve thought for a moment. 'I shall have to give up my nursery job. And that means I shall have to look for another post when I return.'

'You don't have to decide now,' Anita said firmly. 'I know it's come as a shock. I haven't recovered myself yet. Think about it carefully. But let me know as soon as possible because if you don't go I shall have to find someone else.'

Eve knew before she left that evening that she was going to agree to go. It was a heaven-sent opportunity and she would be a fool if she ignored it. And when she saw the look of relief on Amy's face when she mentioned that she would be going away, she knew she had made the right choice. It was not that her sister did not want her to share the flat. The two girls were very close and got on well together. But it was embarrassing for both of them whilst Bill was at loggerheads with Amy.

The head mistress of the school in Kensington had been reasonable and had suggested that she might do with a temporary teacher until Eve returned. And after hearing that, Eve forgot all her qualms and began to prepare for the trip.

She felt Tommy tug at her arm and she opened her eyes guiltily. She had been so immersed in her thoughts that she had forgotten where she was. The air-line hostess was standing beside her, offering her a tray with lunch for the two of them.

'We are well ahead of schedule,' she remarked cheerfully. 'In another hour we ought to be there.'

After that, the time passed quickly. Tommy became rather restless, but Eve did not reprimand him. He had been exceedingly good on the whole. She had expected tears before they left, but he had been too excited to take in the fact that he might not see Anita again. She had kept her emotion well in hand, knowing that she might upset Tommy. Eve had felt very sorry for her. It had been generous of her to take Tommy and she did not think his father had treated Anita well. I suppose men don't understand how attached a woman becomes to a child, Eve thought as she glanced at the boy. He's such a likeable child, with far more confidence than most infants of five. Anita hasn't spoilt him. She's made him rely on himself as much as possible. I suppose she knew that one day she would have to part with him. No doubt his father will marry again. He can't be more than thirty, if that.

Tommy said eagerly, 'They are flashing again!'

Eve nodded. 'Yes. We have to fasten our seat belts. That means we are going to land.'

'I know that!' he exclaimed indignantly.

'It won't be long now before you meet your Daddy.'

'Will he be at the airfield?'

Eve hesitated. 'I'm not sure. It depends whether he has received your aunt's letter. But you needn't worry. I have his address. The airport coach will take us into the city.'

It had not been quite as easy as Eve

13

had expected. She had thought that Dean Rimmer had an apartment in the city, but after making several enquiries she discovered that he lived out in one of the modern suburbs. Confused by the narrow, winding streets, the noise of excitable, exasperating touts who were so persistent, Eve was grateful when a young man spoke to her in English and found a cab for them.

Beneath the hot blue sky the Rimmer house looked like a white square box with deep rectangular slots serving as windows. It was exactly like the other flat-roofed houses in the avenue, separated by trees which were unfamiliar to Eve. She paid off the driver without haggling, knowing full well that he was overcharging her, but she was feeling too exhausted to care. Even Tommy had a wilted air and could scarcely keep his eyes open.

Eve picked up the luggage the cabman had dropped on to the pavement and began to walk towards a gap in the trees. Tommy followed her, then for some unaccountable reason lagged behind. Eve put down the cases and went back to him.

'What's the matter, Tommy?'

'I don't want to go in there. I'm fwightened.'

Eve stopped and put her arms about him. 'There's nothing to be scared of. You will feel better when you're inside. It's this hot sun. You're not used to it.'

Tommy flicked a fearful glance at the blaze of white wall. 'I don't like those black things.'

Eve laughed. 'Don't be silly! That's only lattice-work to cover the windows. They have to prevent people climbing in.'

She went back to the luggage, but did not pick it up, for she heard a car pull up sharply. A tall man dressed in white climbed out and banged the door carelessly. As he strode down the path towards them Eve knew it had to be Tommy's father. His hair was almost as fair as the boy's and his eyes as blue if not bluer.

'Say, now this is a surprise!' The man hesitated, looking at them uncertainly. 'You are Miss Lovell?'

Before Eve could answer he turned to Tommy who was gazing at him expectantly. 'Haven't you anything to say, boy? Aren't you pleased to see me?'

Tommy hung back for a few seconds then made a sudden dive at the man's legs. 'Daddy!' he cried his voice squeaking because he was so excited. 'We came in a big jet. It flew faster than a 'normous big bird!'

'I bet.' Dean swung him up into his arms and hugged him.

Eve watched them, admiring Mr Rimmer's strong, athletic body and clear-cut features. He was as she had supposed, about thirty years old and pleasing to look at. Agreeable also, she told herself with satisfaction. I ought to find him easy to get along with.

Dean had put Tommy down and was smiling at Eve, showing white, even teeth. 'Sorry I wasn't there to meet you. I received Anita's letter only an hour

16

ago. I've just come back from the airport. I missed you by minutes.'

He stared at her as if he had suddenly become aware of the attractive picture she made standing there in her green velvet trouser suit with the sun bronzing her thick dark hair.

'I had expected someone older,' he said. 'Anita said Tommy's teacher was bringing him over.'

Eve smiled. 'Tommy isn't in my class. I teach the babies. But I've known Anita and Tommy for some time. She thought Tommy might be less lonely with me.'

'It was good of you. Come along in. Let's get out of this sun. I guess you could do with a drink.'

He stooped, picked up the luggage, then led the way along the path to a nail-studded door which opened when he pushed it.

Dean turned his head to grin at Eve who was close behind. 'I went out in such a rush I forgot to lock it. I forgot the catch was on.'

Eve glanced at the small hall, where

shaggy Berber rugs covered most of the polished floor. It looked very gay, she thought, but was surprised that it all seemed so small. She had expected a larger, more sumptuous house. Why she was not quite sure.

Dean put down their cases and ushered them into a pale blue living-room. It was deliciously cool in there and Eve found her spirits reviving as she noticed the modern chairs and settee. It all looked so restful, with flowers arranged on the odd small tables and masses of books filling the shelves covering the inner wall.

'What a pleasant room!' she exclaimed as she sank down into a chair. 'The white glare outside is almost too much. But in here everything is subdued.'

'Sure. It's not too bad. I had it redecorated when I came.'

'How long have you been here?' she asked idly, and wondered why he hesitated before replying.

'The lease was for two years. It's nearly up now.'

'Oh as long as that?' She glanced in surprise at the walls, which appeared to have been recently painted.

'If you will excuse me I will go and have a word with my housekeeper. She will be upstairs, preparing the rooms for you. I will ask her to make you some tea.' He smiled. 'You would prefer that, no doubt?'

'Yes, if it's not too much trouble. But I expect Tommy would prefer a soft drink.' Eve got to her feet. 'I can see to it if she's busy.'

'Okay. I will show you where everything is. I want you to feel at home here. If we do it ourselves we can brew a pot of Ceylon tea. Samira would be sure to give us glasses of mint tea. She's real obstinate.'

'Samira is your housekeeper?'

'Sure.' He slanted a swift glance at her. 'She lives in the house, so you won't be alone with me.'

Eve smiled faintly. 'The house must be bigger than it looks. Has it four bedrooms?'

'No, three. I have a small study. I can sleep in there. I thought you might prefer a room to yourself.'

Eve glanced at Tommy, who was wandering about the room inspecting the Moorish pottery and ornaments. 'I think it might be better for Tommy if I share a room with him.'

Dean lifted a dark eyebrow. 'I understood from Anita that he was used to being on his own.'

'He is. But all this is strange to him. He's barely five years old.'

'Okay, if you think that's best. I want the boy to settle down quickly. Was he very attached to Anita?'

'Not as much as if she had been his mother.' She broke off in confusion. 'I'm sorry. I spoke without thinking.'

He waved her apology aside. 'Tommy's mother died three years ago.' He remained silent for a few moments, then said abruptly, 'I will tell Samira to leave my room as it is. I won't be a moment.'

Eve was glancing through a batch of

magazines when he returned.

'I notice they are all American,' she remarked as she put them down and followed him out of the living-room.

'I have them sent over. I didn't want to lose touch.'

'Anita told me you left America some years ago. Have you ever been back?'

'I intend to go back,' he replied.

Aware that he had evaded her question, Eve did not ask him any more. At the time it scarcely registered, but afterwards when she recalled other items it made her curious.

The kitchen was modern, which surprised Eve a little. She was having to modify the fixed ideas she had arrived with.

Noticing her astonishment, Dean drawled, 'Tangier is not as uncivilised as you would suppose. It's become a popular resort and you will find it's much the same as most places with European standards. Only in the old city itself are some things unchanged.'

Eve chuckled. 'I have to confess I had

imagined something quite different.'

Dean grinned. 'A wicked, mysterious, exotic city with dramatic Moorish surroundings? You will find that if you search for it. Allah is still all powerful and you will see veiled women, Berber tribesmen in flowing robes, overladen camels, and mosques and minarets.'

'That's a relief. I hate being disillusioned. Morocco is such a historical country.'

'If you're interested I can fill you in on its history,' Dean said casually as he made the tea in an earthenware pot. 'There's plenty of books in the living-room you might find useful. If you are looking for colour in Tangier you won't be disappointed. You would imagine an artist has daubed the entire city with exotic colour; dawn, sunset, even the earth, the hills and inhabitants.'

Eve had arranged the cups and saucers on a tray and Dean began to pour milk into a yellow jug. He did it carefully, not spilling a drop before he placed the jug on the tray.

'Biscuits or pastries?' he enquired, opening the door of a wall-cupboard.

'Biscuits would be more suitable for Tommy.'

'Okay. Now it's ready. Lead the way.'

Tommy had vanished, but was soon found out on the patio, where he was diligently prodding a tiny lizard who had been sunning himself on the warm stones.

'I've never seen a fwog like that before,' he remarked solemnly.

Dean laughed. 'It's a lizard, a baby one. You will see lots more. Come on in. Eve has some fruit juice for you.'

Tommy drank it quickly, for he was eager to return to the lizard. Eve sat down to enjoy the tea, for she was extremely thirsty, and took the opportunity to study Dean more closely. He was not as bronzed as she had thought he would be after Tommy's description; a fact which puzzled her as he had been in Tangier a long time. He looked more scholarly than she had imagined and this surprised her also. According to Anita, he was the adventurous type and had travelled a good deal. In repose Dean's face reflected an inner calm, more the stamp of a thinker. A strong face, Eve decided as she noted the firm, slightly jutting jaw, the decisive mouth and straight nose. Yes, he's very striking.

Suddenly she became aware that Dean was sizing her up just as critically and she averted her gaze in some confusion.

'It's unusual for you to stay so long in one place, isn't it, Mr Rimmer?' she asked curiously. 'Anita told me you never settled for long but preferred to travel.'

He smiled. 'It sounds as if Anita filled you in pretty well. It's time Tommy had a home of his own. I'm hoping he will appreciate it.'

'You think a home with you will compensate him for the loss of Anita?' Eve knew that she was speaking bluntly, but she had been asked to find out whether there was a chance of happiness for the boy.

'If I hadn't thought so I would not have sent for him.' Dean frowned. 'Arrangements have been made for Tommy to be cared for. It's kind of you to be concerned. I can assure you there is no need for you to worry whether he will be happy or not.'

'I had to ask,' Eve said awkwardly. 'Anita is very fond of the boy. That's why she asked me to come. She will believe me if I send her a good report.'

'There's no need to come to any conclusion yet is there?' Dean smiled. 'First impressions are sometimes wrong.'

Eve laughed ruefully. 'I haven't formed any bad ones. Please don't think I'm being critical. I only know what Anita has told me. It's difficult for a man on his own to bring up a child.'

'Sure, I agree. There's plenty of time to alter that.'

'Do you intend to take him back to America?'

'No,' Dean said sharply, then, as if he regretted his hasty denial, added smoothly, 'Tommy will stay here for three months at least. After that we shall see. As you are going to be with us during his stay I would prefer you to drop the surname. Dean will be adequate.'

Eve smiled and nodded her head. She had been about to ask him what line of business he was in, but refrained. They had been dangerously near a break in their friendly relationship. So far he had said very little about himself, and had made it obvious that he was not prepared to discuss his personal life with her. It was natural, she supposed. He did not know her and she had been probing rather keenly.

Samira came in a few minutes later to inform them that she had finished making up the beds. Her eyes gleamed like black beads in her grave Arab face and she raised her head at a proud angle as she spoke. Eve noticed that there were deep wrinkles about her eyes and mouth, yet her brown forehead was smooth beneath the black hair drawn back so tightly.

Dean introduced her, saying humorously that Samira was the lady who kept a strict eye on his diet, so preventing him from becoming a gourmet.

The Arab woman flashed a haughty glance at him. 'You not care for the food I prepare? I have served other European families. They have not complained.'

'I was joking, Samira,' Dean said quickly. 'You do very well.'

She nodded, looking more satisfied, then turned to Eve, who had been listening with a faint smile on her lips. 'Mr Rimmer is a difficult man to feed. He buries himself in his books and leaves no time to eat his meals.'

'You mean he's a bookworm.'

Samira raised her black eyebrows. 'Is that what you say? My English is not so good.'

'You speak it very well,' Eve assured her. 'How did you learn it?'

Samira shrugged her fat shoulders. 'I work for Europeans a long time. I speak

27

French, too, but not well. It is not easy to cook for a family if I not speak the language.' Her eyes followed Tommy, who had come in from the patio to explore the room again. 'It will be good to have a child in the house. He looks like you, Mr Rimmer. Would he like something to eat?'

'He's had quite a few biscuits.' Eve smiled. 'I think he's too excited to eat anything else right now.'

Dean, who had been sitting on the settee listening to them, asked abruptly, 'What times does he go to bed?'

'Seven o'clock, usually.' Eve glanced at him uncertainly. 'You can alter that if you wish.'

Dean shook his head. 'You do as you think fit. I have no wish to interfere with his routine. We can have dinner at nine. Will that suit you, Samira?'

The woman shrugged. 'It makes no difference. If I wish to go out I will leave a meal ready for you.'

'Real considerate of you,' Dean said dryly.

Samira replied smoothly, 'It was our arrangement, no? I was not to be tied.'

'Sure, that's what we said. Okay, Samira, I'm easy. You please yourself, but do let Miss Lovell know when you are going out.'

Eve said quickly, 'I can see to the meal if Samira wants to go out. I enjoy cooking.'

'That's not the point,' Dean frowned. 'Samira was employed to act as cook-housekeeper. Let's get this straight from the start. I don't want you to take on any more. I guess Tommy can be a full day's occupation.' He stood up and stretched himself. 'I'm going to leave you to settle in. You won't need me around and I have a few things which need attending to.'

Tommy skipped up to him and put his arms around his trousered legs. 'Can I come with you, Daddy?'

Eve noticed the startled expression in Dean's blue eyes and was conscious of acute surprise. It was such a natural thing for the boy to ask. Then it dawned on her that Dean was not used to having a child around, perhaps had not realised what would be expected of him.

Dean detached himself with gentle firmness from Tommy's clinging fingers. 'Not this time, Junior. I will see you at dinner, Eve.'

There was a dead silence for a few minutes after he had gone. Eve felt disappointed that he had not made more of a fuss of the boy. Tommy was beginning to feel disconsolate and Eve sensed how lost he was with only acquaintances around him.

Putting her arm about him, she whispered gently, 'Shall we go and see what it's like upstairs? We can have a wash and change our clothes. Perhaps you could have a short nap.'

'I'm not a baby,' he said sullenly.

Eve smiled. 'Grown-ups enjoy a nap when they are tired. We had a long journey, didn't we? You will have to tell Samira how you came.'

'Don't want to!' Tommy retorted

belligerently and hid behind Eve's green velvet trousers.

'He will feel better in the morning,' the Arab woman stated, ignoring the boy as she turned away.

'He's had too much excitement for one day,' Eve remarked. 'Come along, Tommy. I'm going to take a shower. You can please yourself what you do. You can stay down here with Samira or come with me.'

Tommy clutched at Eve's hand. 'I'm coming with you,' he quavered. Samira's inscrutable face frightened him.

'It's the first door at the top of the stairs,' the housekeeper explained. 'I will bring the grips up for you.'

Dean was scowling as he walked from the house to his car. I'm making a real mess of it, he thought morosely. Why the heck did I tell the girl I had the place painted when I came here? It sticks out a mile that it's been done recently. I hadn't reckoned on Anita sending such an intriguing companion for Tommy. She's a real beaut . . . no mistake about that. Knocked me off course at first . . . real stupid I was . . . especially as the girl's intelligent as well. It would be easier if she was less observant. It's bad enough as it is without this extra worry.

He sighed heavily as he climbed into the car and started the engine. Nadia! Good grief. I'd forgotten her, he thought in alarm. She's going to throw a spanner in the works if I'm not mistaken. How the dickens am I going to cope with two of them? He shook his head and the car jerked away as he changed the gears clumsily. It's real strange . . . before Eve turned up it didn't seem too difficult; far simpler than it does now. Why the heck did I get into this? It's all so complicated. The next three months are going to seem like years. If I could keep away from the house it would be easier . . . but where am I to go? The city is dangerous; too many people . . . Show myself but on no account be contacted! That's a laugh. I doubt whether I shall survive the course. If I escape a fatal accident I'm likely to end up a nervous wreck.

He smiled grimly as he accelerated. No point in having doubts now, he told himself sternly. It's too late. I'm in it up to my neck! His eyes went automatically to his rear mirror. Darn it! I'm being followed. I thought I had shaken off that persistent tail.

With his face set in grim lines, he turned the car into a side road so fast that it skidded dangerously. He righted it skilfully, then settled down to use all his wits to fox the driver of the car which was following him so doggedly.

2

Eve settled in very quickly. She had become so used to making herself scarce at frequent intervals in Amy's flat that she found the freedom of movement in her new home very refreshing.

She met Dean at dinner every evening and sometimes had lunch or breakfast with him. He seemed to keep erratic hours. Used to a routine herself, she found this strange at first, but became used to it after a few days. Dean had an office in the city where he met his clients and conducted deals. But what line of business he was in Eve could not fathom from his conversation. So, feeling curious because she thought she ought to know as much as possible about Tommy's father before she left him in his care, she tackled Samira about it one morning after breakfast.

'I understood he's a salesman. I think you would call him a middle man or agent.' The housekeeper's black eyes revealed her surprise at Eve's ignorance. 'He buys and sells goods. Sometimes it is wine or pottery, even precious stones when he comes across them. It is thought that he deals in arms, too, but that I ought not to speak of. It is only a rumour, you understand. There is much money to be made if you know the right people.'

Eve frowned, wishing that she had not asked. She did not like the hint Samira had dropped about Dean selling arms. 'Have you always been Mr Rimmer's housekeeper?' she enquired.

'No. I have been here two, three months. Before that Mr Rimmer do things for himself.' Samira raised her plump arms in horror. 'If you had seen this house when I came you would believe that.'

'What made you come here?'

'The agency sent me. Mr Rimmer applied for a housekeeper. He said he needed someone because his son was coming to live with him. The decorators were here and the place was in a mess when I arrived.'

Eve looked puzzled. 'I thought Mr Rimmer had lived here a long time.'

'That is so. He has been in Tangier some years. I had heard of him and knew him by sight but had never spoken to him.'

Eve laughed self-consciously. 'You think it strange that I am asking all these questions. You see, I knew nothing about Tommy's father until a week ago.'

'It is natural to ask questions,' Samira replied. 'I, too, am curious about Tommy. I wonder why a man as busy as Mr Rimmer suddenly decided to send for his son. He has not taken much notice of him now he is here.'

Eve secretly agreed with her, but loyalty to her employer made her defend Dean. 'That's because he does not want to alarm the boy. He wants his son to get to know him gradually. He will change. He's promised Tommy several outings. I think Mr Rimmer is being sensible.'

'That may be so.' Samira nodded her head. 'The boy is slow to make friends.'

This was not the case, but Eve did not contradict the woman. Tommy avoided Samira because he was scared of her. Eve sympathised with him, for the Arab woman frightened her sometimes. It was the way her dark eyes seemed to bore into her innermost thoughts when she spoke to her. Eve had the uncanny feeling that the woman knew what she was thinking, although no words were spoken.

Sometimes Dean would drive Eve and Tommy away from the suburbs through the European section, with its tree-lined avenues, to the beach, and leave them there for a few hours to enjoy the three miles of sand and blue sea. So far, Dean had not stayed with them, making various excuses. Sometimes it was a client he had to meet or on other occasions he had to see his accountant, do some interviewing, or get back to his ledger books. All valid excuses as far as Eve could gather. Tommy loved the sea and golden sand, so it was no hardship to go there so frequently, but Eve did find it lonely sometimes. So she was delighted one morning when she came out of the water after a swim to find Tommy holding a conversation with the young man who had found a cab for them the day they had arrived.

'I was hoping I would run into you,' he said, giving her a friendly smile.

Eve pulled off her cap and ran her fingers through her hair. The young man's brown eyes glinted with admiration as he appraised her trim figure in the red-and-white striped swimsuit.

'I haven't had time to acquire a sun-tan,' she said laughingly, feeling self-conscious.

'You look delightful. Your figure is perfect. Why bother about a tan?' He smiled. 'I'm Evan Morgan. I'm a teacher at the English school.'

She looked interested. 'Are your

pupils European?'

'Not all of them. Some lessons I have to use Arabic.'

'Really? That's difficult, isn't it?'

He grinned. 'I thought it might be at first, but I've become accustomed to it. What about you? Are you on vacation?'

Eve shook her head. 'No. I'm looking after Tommy for Mr Rimmer.' She was looking towards the boulevard and noticed Dean ploughing his way towards them. 'He's coming over now to fetch us.'

Evan's face darkened with disappointment. 'That's a pity. I was hoping you would have a drink with me before lunch.'

'I would like to. Perhaps we could make it another day. Mr Rimmer can't always spare the time to bring Tommy and me to the beach. I could walk here I expect, but I haven't been here long enough to find my bearings.'

'I can pick you up in my car,' Evan said eagerly. 'It's only an old banger, but it saves the feet. I have a week's vacation. Can I see you tomorrow?'

'I will ask Mr Rimmer.'

'Ask me what?' Dean enquired, giving the young man a scowling glance.

'Good morning, Mr Rimmer.' Evan smiled at Dean, but received no friendly nod or greeting. He went on awkwardly, 'Don't you remember me? We met at Gloria's cocktail party. We didn't speak to one another, but I was with my sister-in-law's crowd.'

Quick to sense Dean's reluctance to answer, Eve said hurriedly, 'Evan has offered to bring Tommy and me to the beach tomorrow.'

Evan looked at Dean, a half-rueful smile on his lips. 'You are wondering who the deuce I am. You don't recall ever seeing me.'

Dean glanced at him briefly. 'I didn't say so. You are Doctor Morgan's brother, a teacher at the English school.'

'That's right.' Evan smiled with relief. 'Gloria often talks about you. She was saying only the other day that she ought to look you up.'

'Tell her I'm too busy at the moment for social calls.' Dean turned to Eve, who had hastily pulled on a shortie jacket made of red towelling, and thrust her feet into her sandals when she realised that Dean was anxious to go. 'Are you ready, Eve?'

'Yes,' she replied quickly as she finished dusting the sand off Tommy's legs. 'Can you carry Tommy across to the boulevard? I will put his sandals on there.'

'Is it all right for me to call for Eve tomorrow?' Evan asked, unwilling to allow himself to be ignored.

Dean turned his head and nodded. 'If that's what Eve wants, okay. Now we really have to leave.'

Evan walked back with them and watched as they climbed into Dean's car. Dean seemed put out by the attention and Eve found herself feeling uncomfortable and slightly dismayed by his attitude.

'If you don't want me to see Mr

Morgan, it makes no difference to me, Mr Rimmer,' she said quietly as they drove up the hill towards the house.

Dean frowned. 'I have no objection. He's a pleasant enough young man. But don't get me involved. Gloria Morgan has a reputation for being a man-eater.'

Eve chuckled. 'I see! In that case I shall behave very tactfully when your name crops up.'

'I shall rely on your discretion. Did you enjoy yourself, Tommy?'

He listened to the boy's excited chatter with a preoccupied expression on his face and frequently glanced at his rear mirror. He was being tailed by a different make of car today. Dean smiled twistedly to himself, but made no attempt to lose it. Taking his time, he took the direct route back to his house.

Eve had not taken much notice of Evan when he had accosted them on the beach. But the next morning she was struck by his dark good looks. He had black, curly hair, soft brown eyes

42

and a lean, smooth face. He was not very tall, only a couple of inches above herself, but he had a lithe, slim figure with broad shoulders.

'This is a treat for me,' he remarked as he drove Tommy and Eve away from the house. 'There are so few unattached European girls in my circle.' He stopped to give her a quizzical glance. 'You are free, I suppose?'

She laughed. 'If you mean, have I a boy friend, no, I haven't.'

'Good. Very surprising, though. I would have thought you would have had dozens.'

Eve smiled. 'It wouldn't be true to say I haven't had any who were interested. I do meet one or two occasionally, but I've never liked them enough to become serious.'

Catching a glimpse of the sparkling blue waters of the Mediterranean, Evan said suddenly, 'Shall we have a quick spell on the beach? There's so many places I want to take you to. But the sea looks inviting. Afterwards we can have a drink before I show you round the Medina.'

'Tommy will like that.'

Evan chuckled. 'It's not Tommy I'm aiming to please.'

'I shall enjoy anything. I've been planning to have a session in the bazaars, but I'm rather scared of going there alone.'

They stayed on the beach for over an hour, swimming, sun-bathing and watching the graceful yachts skimming the blue waters. Then they took Tommy across the boulevard and had ice-cream and drinks at a sidewalk café.

Glancing at her tiny wrist-watch, Eve said regretfully, 'We haven't time to see the markets or the Sultan's palace. Samira will have lunch ready for us. She doesn't like us to be late.'

'We can go tomorrow,' Evan said eagerly. 'Perhaps we could go there first before your swim.'

Eve hesitated. 'I shall have to ask Mr Rimmer. I am employed to look after Tommy.'

'Very well. I will call for you about

nine o'clock. If you can't go we will make it another day.'

'Aren't we messing up your vacation?'

Evan laughed. 'Far from it. I never know what to do with myself. I've explored most of the city and have taken trips out into the desert. I can't trust my old banger to go too far. Gloria is a great one for organising trips. My brother, being a doctor, has long hours, five a.m. to nine p.m. usually, so his wife has far too much time on her hands. She's taken me to Tetouan, Fez and Rabat. Now she's planning to go to Marrakesh.'

'Marvellous names, aren't they? Before I came here I imagined Morocco to be flat, but Tangier is built on the hills, seven, I believe.'

'You had forgotten the Atlas mountains and the Rif. They practically seal off the north. In the south they have severe droughts, floods and sometimes snow near the Sahara. The climate is not so favourable. The mountains make a tremendous difference between north and south.'

'Mr Rimmer has told me a little of its history. He becomes very enthusiastic when he's describing the impact of the Spanish and French on the country.'

'The English, Arabs, Jews and Moors had a hand in it, too.' Evan grinned. 'It's a complicated set-up. No wonder there's so much intrigue in Moroccan cities.'

'Having Algeria on its borders can't help,' Eve said thoughtfully.

Evan's brown eyes twinkled. 'If you're planning a hasty escape, let me remind you that dear old Gib is just across the water.'

Eve laughed. 'How well you read my thoughts!' She pushed Tommy's empty glass away from him. 'It's time to go,' she said firmly.

Eve felt rather flat when Evan's vacation came to an end and she was left to herself once more. Thinking that it might be a good idea to give Tommy a few lessons, she began to spend the first hour each morning after breakfast sitting on the flat roof with Tommy. It was cool then and both of them were more able to cope with the lessons Eve prepared the evening before. Dean thought it an excellent arrangement and often spent some time with them. He listened with interest as Eve explained the meaning of the pictures in the books she had brought with her and was surprised that the boy could read so well.

'It's unusual at that age, isn't it?' he asked.

Eve smiled. 'Yes, it certainly is. Tommy is very quick. I never have to repeat anything more than twice.'

'I've known other bright kids, but none of them could read at five.'

'I think it's because he's never had other children to play with. Anita was strict with him. He had a regular routine and she would not allow him to go to other children's homes after school. Tommy was thrown on his own resources. He always had plenty of books and luckily he seemed to enjoy them.'

Dean frowned. 'It sounds as if he was a lonely child.'

'Please don't blame Anita. I think she was over careful because Tommy was not her child. Also she had a job to go to in the daytime. She loved him and that's the most important thing.'

Dean smiled. 'He was lucky to have you. I wonder if you know how good you are at your work? It's been real inspiring, listening to you.'

Eve smiled faintly. 'If you enjoy what you are doing, that helps. I'm not really a good teacher. I don't know enough.'

'Who does? But one learns all the time. Having the aptitude is a necessity for any teacher.'

Eve glanced at him curiously. 'You say that as if you've tried teaching yourself.'

'Did I?' Dean replied carelessly. 'I guess I got carried away. I was merely putting myself in your place.'

'You have good reason to be very

proud of your son,' Eve told him seriously, and was surprised at the blank expression on his face.

'I'm thankful he's going to come into his own at last,' he said enigmatically. 'I've taken up too much of your time. I shall have to be off. See you tonight, Eve.'

One morning after Eve had been in Morocco two weeks Dean came up on to the roof, looking more relaxed than he usually did. He was wearing white slacks, a dark blue sports shirt, and had a camera slung over his shoulder.

'Any objection to skipping the lesson today, Eve?' he asked. 'I thought we might take a drive round and inspect some of the old legations. They aren't used now, unfortunately. Then perhaps we could visit the markets and Kasbah.'

Eve's eyes sparkled. 'Yes, that would be lovely! The morning is the best time because Tommy is fresher.'

'You don't need to change, do you?' Dean was looking at her pale green linen dress. 'How do you always manage to look so right?'

'I didn't know I did. I put this sleeveless dress on because it's cool.'

'You know which colours suit you best. Leaf green, isn't it? It looks great with your dark hair and green eyes.'

For a second or two Eve was at a loss for words. She was astonished that he had noticed the colour of her eyes. Tommy had disappeared downstairs to put on his sandals and they were alone on the roof top.

Dean did not appear to be in a hurry to go. 'I'm very grateful to you, Eve,' he said in a low voice. 'I can't begin to tell you what it means to know I have someone like you looking after Tommy. I have to own that I was real nervous at the thought of having him here. But both of you have fitted in so well. There have been no scenes, no bouts of homesickness, and I'm sure it's all due to you.'

Eve smiled. 'Not entirely. Give Tommy his due also, Mr Rimmer. He is an amiable child.'

'Mr Rimmer!' Dean looked at her reproachfully. 'I told you to cut that out. I'm fully aware of Tommy's good points. But I've watched you dealing with him. You sense immediately when something is bothering him and instantly do something about it. I never understood before how much attention young children need. You deal with upsets with all the calmness of a saint.'

She chuckled. 'Please, Mr . . . sorry, Dean! That's going too far. I'm a school teacher. I'm used to having children around me.'

'Thanks for remembering the Dean bit. I'm twenty-eight, Eve, not a middle-aged man.'

The intimacy in his voice was so unnerving that Eve automatically moved to the edge of the roof so that she was farther away from him. She pretended an interest in the view and glanced up the hill to the ancient walls and minarets of the city. Then, as she looked down, she saw Samira in the avenue. The housekeeper was talking to two men who had their faces almost hidden by the hoods of their *burnouses*. Consumed with curiosity, Eve leaned over to acquire a better view and screamed as she felt herself overbalance.

Dean rushed forward and pulled her back. She was trembling and unthinkingly fell into his arms, thankful for the feeling of security. Suddenly he bent his head and his lips sought hers. For a second or two she was unable to resist as a fierce passion consumed them both. Then, with her mind in a daze, she drew back and he released her.

'You will have to be careful,' Dean said, his voice hoarse with emotion. 'I believed you were going to fall. I was terrified! You could have killed yourself! It's a long drop to the ground.'

Eve glanced at him, then looked away, too confused to speak of that embrace or what it could mean. She was shocked at herself for not resisting it.

'It was stupid of me,' she said shakily.

Dean had pulled himself together and was smiling at her nervousness. 'If it had been Tommy I wouldn't have been surprised.'

'I've told him enough times to keep away from the edge,' Eve said ruefully. 'Please don't mention it to him. It would undermine my authority.'

'I won't, I promise you. Eve . . . ' Dean broke off, giving her a searching glance. But whatever it was he was going to say he changed his mind, for Tommy was coming up the stairs.

'We might as well go down,' he remarked. 'Coming, Eve?'

Samira came from the kitchen as they reached the hall. 'Will you be in to lunch, Mr Rimmer?' she enquired.

Dean turned to Eve. 'Shall we get something out? Yes, it will make a change. Don't prepare anything, Samira.'

As the woman turned away Eve caught a gleam of triumph in the bead-like eyes. She wondered about it as she followed Dean and Tommy out of the house. She had never felt at ease with the housekeeper because she found difficulty in getting a response from her. Once Samira had asked questions about Eve's way of life, but she shut up like a clam when Eve asked her about herself. Eve had shrugged off her misgivings, telling herself that it was because they were of different races. But today that expression in Samira's dark eyes made her extremely curious. It was not as if she had much to do in the house. And she had all the time off she wanted.

But Eve quickly forgot the house-keeper once they were all in Dean's car. He drove them towards the bay, then along the promenade, pointing out the large, modern hotels which had sprung up in recent years. Then he took them to see the legations which had been so active a few years ago and were now empty or used for other purposes. Some of the gardens were superb, but others were overgrown with shrubs and plants and looked uncared for.

Dean was an interesting guide, for he

knew so much of the history of the Moroccan city. The time flew by. They had lunch in the Hammadi, a restaurant in the Rue de la Kasbah, then parked the car and walked to the Medina. The winding streets were crowded with bearded men in flowing robes, Arab women — some veiled, others with only the lower part of their faces hidden above their graceful kaftans — beggars, wearing torn and dirty jeans or ragged pantaloons, and noisy, excited tourists. There was more than enough to keep Tommy enthralled and they had difficulty in luring him away from the snake charmers and acrobats.

At one point during the afternoon Eve became separated from Dean and the boy. She had been admiring the lengths of satins and silks on one stall and when she turned she found herself face to face with a woman in a bright blue kaftan. She had a head scarf pulled up over her face and only her eyes were revealed. Although the woman made no sign of recognition and swiftly turned away, Eve recognised her. It was Samira. Eve would have known those glittering black eyes anywhere. Puzzled, she stood watching the figure in the blue kaftan until it disappeared into a tiny shop where rugs and carpets were on display.

When Dean found her she mentioned that she had seen his housekeeper.

'That's quite probable,' he drawled. Then, noticing how disturbed she was looking, added, 'Has something upset you?'

She smiled. 'I expect I'm being silly. It's just a feeling I have. We were so close, yet Samira deliberately ignored me. Her face was nearly covered, so she might have thought I hadn't noticed her.'

'She often wears a kaftan and covers her face.' Dean frowned. 'Funny she didn't speak to you. Did you notice where she went? Don't point or turn round, just tell me.'

Eve nodded. 'Just behind you there is

a row of shops all jammed together. She went into the carpet shop. That was some minutes ago. I haven't seen her come out.'

Dean turned slowly and carelessly eyed the place she had spoken of, then he put his arm in hers and began to move away rapidly, holding Tommy with his other hand.

'Do you know something about that place?' Eve gasped as she tried to keep up with him.

Dean slowed down, then stopped. 'Yes, I do. I'm real surprised. I had thought that Samira was just what she said she was, a housekeeper.'

'I don't understand. What else could she be?'

Dean smiled grimly. 'Something unpleasant. It was too much to expect, I guess. I ought to have taken it for granted. It would have been too easy. Now I am bothered.' He hesitated, glancing at Tommy, who had strolled away to join the crowd about a man who was performing conjuring tricks.

'We may as well stay here for a few minutes. I'm glad you told me about Samira. She's gone in there to give her report. I ought to have guessed that she has been planted in our household.'

'Do you mean she's been spying on us? Why would she do that?'

Dean looked worried. 'I'm sorry, Eve. I can't explain. Only from now on do be careful what you say to Samira.'

Eve said dryly, 'That won't be difficult. I've never said very much to her. She's not an easy person to get on with.'

'Has she asked any questions about me?'

'Not really. She did ask me if I had known you before I came here. She seemed more curious about what I did.'

'Yes, she would want to know.'

Eve frowned. 'Dean, what is all this about? Wouldn't it be wiser for me to know?'

'No,' he said emphatically. 'It would be dangerous.' He walked across to Tommy and, ignoring his protests, pulled him away from the conjurer. 'Let's get away from here. We can have an hour on the beach before we go back.'

Samira had been almost as startled as Eve and had pulled up her head scarf, hoping that the English girl had not noticed her. Hurrying through the crowds, she glanced furtively behind her before she made a dive for the carpet shop, and she was breathing heavily as she mounted the stairs, a short, narrow flight at the rear of the shop, hidden by gauze curtains.

Without knocking she entered a foul-smelling room and glanced about her. Two men, one bearded, wearing red *tarbooshes* decorated with blue silk tassels which dangled over their white *jellabahs*, were lounging on cushions on the floor. Both were smoking *hookahs* and showed no interest at her sudden appearance. But Samira was well used to their indifference. She was a woman and her upbringing had taught her to wait patiently until she was spoken to.

The man with the beard cast a piercing look at her. 'You have news, woman?'

'It is the same as before.'

'No one has come to the house?'

'Only the school teacher, Evan Morgan.'

'What does he talk about?'

'Very little. He is interested in the young woman.'

'Have you found out about her?'

'She is here to look after the boy.'

'You said that before. Have you listened to her conversation with Rimmer?'

'I have. She knows nothing.'

'Have you opened the mail?'

'There has been nothing except magazines from America.'

The other, younger man stood up, revealing a European suit beneath his loose, white *jellaba*. 'Are you certain? He has had no letter from Fez?'

'I am. There has been no letter.'

'The woman doctor is cautious,' the bearded man remarked.

The other smiled. 'Our warnings have had a result, Abdul. It is good. Rimmer can do nothing until he hears from her.'

Abdul nodded. 'You can go, woman, but return at once if your suspicions are aroused.'

Samira took the few Moroccan francs he offered her and left. When Dean, with Eve and Tommy, returned to the house in the suburbs Samira was wearing European dress and was preparing the dinner in the kitchen.

Eve noticed that Dean was very quiet during dinner. Tommy had gone to bed soon after they had arrived home, for Eve had found him yawning over his supper. She felt tired herself, for they had been out nearly all day.

After she had taken the coffee cups out to Samira, Eve returned to the living-room and wandered over to the bookcase to select something to read. But she could not concentrate on the volume she had chosen and found her gaze straying across to Dean, who was deep in his book. The incident on the roof was foremost on her mind and it worried her more than a little. She had been kissed before, but had never felt so exhilarated that she had no thought of the expediency of the circumstances. She did not blame Dean. It had been a natural reaction because he was thankful that he had prevented her from falling off the roof. But she could not excuse herself. If it had been a light, meaningless embrace she would not have thought twice about it, but it was her response that frightened and disturbed her. She guessed from Dean's attitude that he had forgotten all about it and found some comfort in that.

Dean had been watching her for some time and when he spoke she glanced at him in a startled fashion. 'Sorry,' she murmured. 'What did you say?'

He smiled. 'You were miles away.' He put his book on the arm of the chair. 'Do you find it lonely here, Eve?'

'Sometimes,' she confessed candidly.

'I'm sorry about this afternoon. It spoilt your day.'

'No, it didn't.' She hesitated, then asked, 'Are you going to give Samira her notice?'

He shook his head. 'No. That wouldn't settle anything. Another agent would take her place. Better the devil I do know. Don't you agree?'

'I was very shocked. It's a horrible thing to do.'

'Don't blame her too much. Circumstances would influence her. I guess she's had so much poverty in her life that she has to use her wits to improve her lot. The money would be useful.'

'Why should anyone want to know what you are doing? I mean . . . to go to so much trouble to find out what happens in this house! I've had the feeling something was wrong, yet could not place it.'

Dean said seriously, 'I guessed it wouldn't be long before you sensed trouble.' He smiled faintly. 'Have you been suspecting me, Eve?'

She laughed as if embarrassed. 'No. But to be quite honest, I have been puzzled. You rarely answer my questions directly and it seems strange that you haven't much of a tan.'

He looked startled. 'Does it show that much?'

'Perhaps others might not notice. Evan hasn't mentioned it. It was Tommy telling me how bronzed his daddy was that caused me to be surprised. Children do exaggerate. I told myself that.'

'It was a stupid omission. Details are so important. I haven't acquired much of a tan because I don't go out more than is necessary.'

Eve's eyes were puzzled. 'Are you in danger? Is that why you don't go far from the house?'

'I could be. I do have to be careful.' He smiled crookedly. 'Don't look so scared! I'm not hiding from the law.'

She breathed a faint sigh of relief. 'That's something, I suppose.'

Dean got to his feet and strode across

to the door. He opened it, listened for a few seconds, then returned to his chair. 'Samira is washing the dishes, so it's safe to talk, but keep your voice low.'

'Yes,' she agreed, waiting expectantly.

He looked at her thoughtfully for a few moments, then leaned forward and spoke earnestly. 'I sure would like to tell you what it's all about, but I can't, not at this stage. Yet what happened today, plus your observations, has convinced me that it's imperative that I safeguard your future and Tommy's.' He frowned. 'I want you to promise me something, Eve.'

'Anything, if it will help,' she replied.

'It has occurred to me that if something went wrong, you might find yourself in a dickens of a situation. Say I was to go out one day and not return, you wouldn't know what to do.'

'Is that likely to happen?' Eve's green eyes were full of dismay.

'It's possible, but I can't see that it would suit anyone's purpose. But the situation could change rapidly. If I do disappear, wait three days, then pack your cases and take Tommy across to Switzerland. I will tell you the address and you can memorise it. It wouldn't be safe to write it down.'

Eve said, looking slightly dazed, 'What do I do when I get there?'

'Wait until someone contacts you. If no one comes after a month has passed, return to England.'

'Wouldn't it be more sensible to go directly to England?'

'No. It's important that you try to make contact with Tommy in Switzerland. Hotel Mignon, Montreux. Think you can remember that?'

'Yes, it's very simple.'

Dean sighed and leaned back in his chair. 'I feel happier now. I doubt whether anything will happen, but it's best to be ready. Tomorrow I will give you enough dollars to cover the trip and pay for a month's board. Dollars will be easier to cash for the *dirham* isn't allowed to be taken out of the country.

Hide the money away in your room.'
He put his finger to his lips as he heard
a noise outside the room.

Eve said loudly, 'If you will excuse
me, Mr Rimmer, I will go and see how
Tommy is.'

'Okay.' Dean nodded and smiled. 'I
shall have an early night also. Sightseeing sure can be tiring.'

Eve opened the door just in time to
see the kitchen door closing. She
turned back into the room and said
softly, 'I'm sure she didn't hear
anything.'

'To be on the safe side we won't
mention this again. You understand
what you have to do?'

'Yes, Dean.' She paused, then added
quickly, 'Whatever it is you are involved
in, I do hope it goes well for you.'

Dean got up and moved to her side.
He put his hand on her shoulder and
pressed it gently.

'Thanks, Eve,' he said gruffly. 'I wish
I could tell you how much you have
done for me already. Perhaps one

day . . . ' He broke off and smiled crookedly. 'No, that would be tempting Allah. Off to bed with you before I break any more resolutions!'

3

Dean's house lay to the east of the port and the Medina and sometimes Eve had difficulty in remembering she was in Tangier. That was until she went up on to the flat roof and cast a glance westward and to the north, where on a clear day she could see across the bay and the Straits of Gibraltar. Because of its sheltered position, the harbour attracted boats of all shapes and sizes, and every day she watched the yachts going out.

There was a regatta once a week and Evan usually made a point of taking her to see it. And when he had a free afternoon he would take her to the Country Club, where they could play tennis while Tommy amused himself playing with the other children.

'I can't understand why Dean doesn't bring you here,' Evan remarked one Saturday afternoon as they strolled off the court with the intention of finding iced drinks to quench their thirst. 'I know he's a member and he has heaps of friends here. They are beginning to wonder what's the matter with him.'

Eve chuckled. 'I haven't noticed anything. I know he has a mountain of work to get through. He looks tired when he returns in the evening. I'm not surprised that he prefers to stay in.'

Evan smiled as he took the racket from her. 'I might be tempted to do the same with you for company. He's not so strange after all.'

'If you imagine we spend long evenings together you are mistaken,' she said seriously. 'I have Tommy to see to and after dinner I go up to my room. Dean reads for a while and then he goes to bed. None of us are up after eleven o'clock.'

'Good Lord! Doesn't he ever take you out?'

'Not in the evenings. He does take an afternoon off sometimes. One day we drove to La Montagne, which used to be a pirates' lair in the seventeenth century.'

'Not much to see there now. It's an expensive residential sector.'

'I know, but there is a wonderful view from the top and there are two palaces which used to belong to the sultans. From there we went on to the Roman ruins on the Asilah road.'

Evan said moodily, 'I wish I had thought of taking you there.'

'I was surprised that Dean was so enthusiastic. He knows an awful lot about Morocco.'

'He ought to. He's lived here long enough.'

'It's more than general knowledge. He could tell me what happened years and years ago. He was so intrigued with the ruins I thought we would never leave.'

'He was trying to impress you,' Evan said scornfully. 'He has seen them before. No one is that interested the second or third time.'

Eve frowned. 'I hadn't thought of

that. Of course, he's used to sightseeing.'

'Forget Dean and his idiosyncrasies! I'm dying of thirst and talking is not a remedy.'

It was only a few days after Eve's last visit to the Country Club that Gloria made a sudden call at the house. Dean had come in unexpectedly to take tea with Eve and Tommy. Samira was out and Eve was setting a table out on the patio when Dean walked in.

'This looks real nice,' he drawled, giving her a warm smile. 'Do you mind if I join you?'

'No. Tommy will be pleased. He's gone up to the bathroom to wash himself.'

Dean chuckled. 'Show himself to the soap and water you mean.'

He had scarcely finished speaking when the doorbell rang. Eve moved towards the french windows, intending to go to the door, but Dean put a warning hand on her arm.

'Wait!' he said. 'I will see who it is first.'

Hurrying to the edge of the patio, he pulled back a thickly leafed branch of a tree and peered through at the path which led up to the door. Then quickly he went back to Eve.

'It's Gloria Morgan,' he muttered. 'I don't want to see her. Tell her I'm at the office.'

'Very well, but where are you going to hide?'

'I can scramble through into the next garden. Get rid of her as quickly as you can and say as little as possible.'

Eve looked at him in dismay. 'I shall have to ask her to stay for tea. She will see the table.'

Dean sighed. 'Okay. I will make myself scarce until dinner.'

The bell rang again and Eve walked through the living-room and out into the hall. She paused for a few moments to give Dean time to escape before she opened the door. A tall, smartly dressed woman in a royal blue trouser suit with a gaily patterned blouse eyed Eve with undisguised indignation.

'I was beginning to think you were all deaf in this house. I know Dean is at home. I saw his car outside.' She stared at Eve, who was taking a few minutes to recover. 'Well, don't stand there, let me in!'

'Yes . . . sorry about the delay. Do come in,' Eve said politely as she stepped aside to allow Gloria to enter.

Tommy dashed down the stairs, but stopped at the bottom when he saw Gloria, apparently fascinated by the woman's halo of golden hair. It ought to have softened her hard features, but only served to draw attention to her dry, sun-tanned skin.

'Is this Dean's son?' she demanded. 'I heard he had arrived.'

'Yes.' Eve smiled at the small boy. 'Tommy, come and say 'hello' to Mrs Morgan.'

Gloria glanced at Eve in some astonishment. 'You know my name?'

Realising that she had slipped up, Eve said awkwardly, 'Evan pointed you out to me one day.'

The woman nodded. 'Yes. He's spoken about you. Tell Dean I'm here, will you?'

'Mr Rimmer doesn't come home during the day.'

'There's no need to make excuses. I'm an old friend. He will see me.'

Tommy suddenly found his tongue and Eve could have hugged him. 'My Daddy's at work,' he said in his high-toned childish voice.

'He can't be! I saw his car outside. Dean never walks if he can avoid it.'

'He did today,' Eve told her firmly. 'Tommy and I were just about to have our tea out on the patio. Would you care to join us, Mrs Morgan?'

'I might as well,' Gloria said begrudgingly. 'I left an important meeting to come here.'

'I am sorry. Mr Rimmer will be disappointed to hear he missed you. I have to bring in the tea. Would you take a seat and make yourself comfortable?' Eve smiled at her politely.

When she returned Gloria was sitting on a chair eyeing herself critically in a small hand mirror. She put it away swiftly when she saw Eve.

'Evan has been raving about you. I thought he was exaggerating. But I can understand now why Dean has been avoiding all his old friends,' Gloria remarked with a hint of spite in her rich, deep voice.

Eve smiled faintly as she put down the teapot. 'You are mistaken if you think I'm the reason. I'm only here to look after Tommy until he settles down with his father. Mr Rimmer is devoting himself to his son. That's why he's neglecting his social life. I shall be returning to England in a couple of months.'

'You don't expect me to swallow that!' Gloria gave her an arrogant stare. 'I'm not that stupid.'

She was being blunt and rude and Eve found it difficult to control her own tongue. Resentment caused her hand to shake as she poured out the tea.

'Evan has told me what a busy life you lead,' she said, making an effort to speak unemotionally. 'Have you lived in Tangier very long?'

'Yes, some time. Hasn't Dean mentioned me?'

'Once or twice. He doesn't say much to me about his friends.'

Gloria sipped her tea, waved Eve's offer of a pastry aside, and asked abruptly, 'Why not?'

Eve smiled. 'You will have to ask Mr Rimmer. As I told Evan, I have very little to do with him. Tommy is my only concern. I spend my days and evenings with him.'

'The nights are free, I assume,' Gloria said insolently. 'Are you alone in this house with Dean and Tommy?'

Eve, conscious that her cheeks were burning, prayed that she was not revealing her anger and resentment. 'No. We have a housekeeper. She sleeps in,' she said flatly. 'There are only three bedrooms, so I sleep in Tommy's room.'

'There was no need to give it to me in detail,' the woman sounded irritated. 'I haven't come to pry.'

What have you come for, then? Eve thought as she cut a pastry for Tommy and told him to eat it slowly.

Breaking the silence which seemed to have fallen upon them, Eve asked quietly, 'Would you like another cup of tea, Mrs Morgan?'

'No, thank you. I've lived here so long I prefer mint tea.'

Eve swallowed. 'If you had mentioned it before I could have made you some.'

'Don't bother. I'm not staying. When you see Dean tell him I'm very annoyed with him. I've been treated badly before, but never ignored. I won't forgive him in a hurry.'

Gloria got up and walked towards the french windows. From the moment she had arrived she had ignored Tommy, so Eve did not ask him to get up to see the woman off. Eve followed her to the front door, managed a cool, polite 'goodbye' and sighed with relief when she was able to shut the woman out.

What insolence! she thought indignantly. How could Dean ever become involved with her! Whatever the relationship had been, he had seen the danger signals in time. Given half a chance Gloria would bulldoze herself into a man's life and take over greedily and without so much as a 'thank you'.

Tommy noticed Eve's set expression when she sat down and looked at her in bewilderment. 'She didn't stay long. Why was she so 'cwoss'? Can I have another pastry?'

'Yes, help yourself,' Eve replied absent-mindedly. She never allowed him to have more than one, for the mixture of honey and almond plus the sugary pastry was very indigestible.

Tommy wriggled with delight as he did as she suggested and quickly had his face covered with sugar. Eve noticed and felt annoyed with herself for giving way.

'If you feel sick afterwards, don't expect me to feel sorry for you.'

Tommy looked up at her, his blue

eyes wide with surprise. 'You are 'cwoss' too, Eve.' He pushed the half-eaten pastry away. 'I won't have any more.'

Eve smiled. 'You're a good boy, Tommy. I'm not cross.'

She took him up to the bathroom to wash the sticky streaks from his face, then went to the kitchen to rinse the teacups.

When Dean met her at dinner his first remark was, 'How did you get on? Did Gloria suspect I was here?'

'I don't think so. She was suspicious at first. She assumed you were home because your car was outside. I told her you walked to your office today.'

Dean smiled. 'It doesn't matter what she thinks. She didn't see me.'

'She wasn't in a very good mood,' Eve remarked, helping herself to a glass of Vichy water before she tackled the *harira* the housekeeper had cooked.

Dean was not keen on Moroccan food and toyed with the thick soup made of eggs, meat and peas. 'Why the heck does Samira give us this?' he said irritably. 'She knows I can't stand it.'

Eve glanced at him in surprise. He was rarely bad tempered and usually joked about Samira's cooking.

'I have told her not to cook it,' she said quietly.

'She takes no notice because she knows she won't be with us much longer.'

'You do intend to get rid of her, then?'

'Not yet, but I guess she won't want to stay too long, so she cooks what she prefers. Getting back to Gloria . . . did she leave any messages?'

Eve smiled. 'She insisted that I tell you that she's very annoyed with you and she dislikes being ignored.' She paused, then continued, choosing her words carefully, 'Evan said that you are well known at the Country Club and your friends are wondering why you no longer go there.'

'I bet they are!' Dean smiled grimly. 'What excuse did you give Gloria?'

'I told her you were devoting your time to Tommy.'

'Good. That ought to satisfy her.'

Eve said bravely, 'It's not exactly true, is it?'

He raised his eyebrows quizzically. 'Why did you say that?'

'You did ask me to stay until Tommy has become used to you. At the rate you are progressing it will take years. You scarcely see Tommy. You leave as soon as he is up and when you return in the evening he's in bed.'

He was silent so long that she said nervously, 'I'm sorry, Dean. I ought not to have criticised you like that.'

'I don't mind.' He smiled at her downcast face. 'You see, I can understand how puzzled you are. I wish I could explain. Thanks for dealing with Gloria for me. And if you could be patient for a little longer I would be grateful.'

'I'm not anxious about myself,' Eve said slowly.

'Tommy is happy, isn't he?'

'Oh, yes,' she said quickly. 'He's used to being on his own. I don't suppose he's noticed that anything is different. He loves the sand and the sun and especially the umbrellas. He finds them amusing.'

'I thought he was more interested in the donkeys.'

'He is, but he becomes upset when he sees them weighed down with panniers filled with heavy goods. Sometimes the poor things can scarcely move.'

'They are strong little animals.'

'I told him that, but he wasn't impressed. One morning he charged at an Arab boy who was striking a donkey with a stick. If Evan hadn't pulled Tommy away there would have been a fight.'

'Evan . . . ' Dean glanced at her thoughtfully. 'You've seen him fairly frequently. Is it because you like him or is he cut from the same cloth as his sister-in-law?'

'He's not so objectionable as Gloria!' She smiled apologetically. 'Sorry, but you did ask me.'

'You needn't apologise. I agree with you about Gloria. So you do enjoy Evan's company!'

'He's very obliging and kind. I was nervous at first about taking Tommy out, but Evan soon put me at ease. Actually parts of the city on the fashionable side are very European.'

Samira came in with the dessert, a very sweet fruit salad. Eve left most of hers. She would have preferred the melon, orange and grapes without the sickly sauce the woman had poured over it. But she did not mention it to Samira because she had discovered that most of the fruit in Tangier was tasteless and guessed that it had become the custom to disguise it with honey, almonds and sugar.

'Ugh! Much more of that and I would be ill,' Dean exclaimed as he followed Eve to the other side of the living-room. Eve had taken the dishes out to the kitchen and had come in with the coffee.

It was the time she looked forward to. With Tommy in bed, she could safely sit down and relax. Dean did not embarrass her, for he usually buried himself in a book. Eve liked to sit there with him, completely at ease and lulled by a deep sense of security. But this evening something had disrupted their peaceful relationship. Instead of sipping her coffee contentedly and musing over the pleasant day she had had, her mind would keep returning to Gloria.

Evidently Dean was in much the same state, for he threw himself into a chair and did not attempt to read.

'If it wasn't for Gloria and the others I could be taking you out to some of the restaurants and other entertainments,' he said moodily. 'Tangier wakes up at night.'

Eve glanced at him curiously. 'Is Gloria the reason why you don't go to the Country Club?'

'She is one reason.'

'I can't believe you would ever become friendly with a woman like that!' She broke off, thinking she had revealed her thoughts too plainly.

He gave her a queer, rueful look. 'Has Gloria been filling in the details? Don't judge me too harshly, Eve. I don't know her all that well.'

Eve said slowly, 'That wasn't the impression she gave me. She spoke as if you and she were on the point of . . . '

'Liaison?' Dean chuckled and there was a glint in his blue eyes which Eve found very disconcerting.

What has got into me? she asked herself with a sense of shock. Dean's private life is his concern, not mine. Why doesn't he tell me so instead of appearing to be amused. Amused yet annoyed both at the same time. It's very confusing!

It was not until she felt his hand pressing into her shoulder that she realised he had got up and moved across to her. He looked very serious and she was astonished when he leaned over and brushed his lips against her smooth forehead. It was over in a second, for he straightened quickly. Amazed at the rush of elation which was making her cheeks burn and her heart pound, Eve was unable to move or speak.

'I hate to see you upset, honey. You needn't worry that pretty head about Gloria,' he drawled in a low voice which carried a hint of tenderness in its depth. He touched her dark head lightly with caressing fingers, then turned away and went from the room.

Eve closed her eyes and leaned back against the chair. For days now she had been conscious of something wonderful happening to her. Ever since that incident on the roof she had been in a kind of dream world, unconscious of past or future. But dreams dissolve and the caress bestowed that evening had made her aware of the foolishness she had been indulging in. She did not think for a moment that Dean was sharing the sweet intoxication of a new love. He was a kind man and the light kiss and touch on the head was much the same as he would give to Tommy. I never thought that falling in love could be so painful, she thought, because that's what is the matter with me. Dean is ever present in my thoughts, day and night. My days are coloured by the looks he gives me; the sudden smile or trivial compliment. Dean likes me . . . Does he feel the same way as I do?

For a second or two her happiness spilled over and the room was suffused with such radiance that her eyes were dazzled. Allowing her imagination to run riot, she pictured what the future could hold. Then, as reason returned, the light went from her face and she became subdued. It's too much to hope for, she muttered. He has known me such a short while.

She could not bear the idea of talking to anyone and, scared that Samira might come in for the coffee cups, she hurriedly left the living-room and went up to her room. But it was a long time before she fell asleep. There were burning tears behind her closed eyelids and a tight feeling in her throat and chest. I'm frightened, she thought in surprise. It's happened so quickly. Perhaps if I think it's hopeless it will happen. I'm too superstitious to take anything for granted.

Eve had been wise to treat her new-found happiness with caution, as she soon discovered when she met Dean again. He seemed very pre-occupied and totally unaware of any intimacy in their relationship. It is as I thought, Eve told herself regretfully. His actions had no hidden meaning. I was foolish to think otherwise.

Another two weeks passed all too swiftly and Eve reminded herself that she had been in Tangier two months. Only four weeks left, she thought discon-solately as she went down to breakfast with Tommy. Dean had nearly finished, but poured himself another cup of coffee so that he could prolong the meal.

'Why you dressed like that?' the boy asked as he dive-bombed his spoon into his grapefruit.

'That's not the way to behave,' Dean said sternly. 'You might have spoilt Eve's dress!'

'Sorry,' Tommy mumbled.

'No damage done, luckily,' Eve assured him cheerfully as she glanced down at her strawberry-pink dress. She would have been upset if it had been soiled because she had pressed it only the evening before and the embroidered lace at the neck and sleeves had been difficult to iron. But because it was a pretty dress she had thought it worth the trouble.

'I'm going riding with Ali-ben-Ahmed this morning,' Dean explained, giving Tommy a smile.

'Can we go with you?'

'I'm afraid not. I planned it some time ago. But if you are good I might ask Ali if you and Eve could see his house one day.'

'Does he live in a *Kasbah*?' Tommy asked between mouthfuls.

Eve and Dean laughed. 'No,' Dean said. 'He lives in a semi-modern house in the residential area a few miles from town.'

Tommy lost interest after that. 'Don't bother,' he said. 'I don't like visiting.'

'Why not?' Dean was giving him a puzzled stare.

'Cos Eve makes me dress up and I have to be nice to everyone.'

'It's good for you. I guess, young man, you are becoming real spoiled. Eve gives in to you too much.'

'She doesn't! Eve always makes me do things I don't want to do.'

Eve chuckled. 'Be careful, Tommy. Your Daddy will think I ill-treat you.'

Dean smiled. 'I guess I needn't lose any sleep over that. You will have to be disciplined sometimes, Tommy. This is just an interlude. Make the most of it.' He threw down his table napkin and stood up. 'I'm tempted to stay and talk but I do have things to see to. What are you going to do today?'

He looked so handsome in his riding outfit that Eve's voice caught in her throat as she tried to reply. But luckily

Tommy answered his question eagerly.

'We are going on a bus to the Avenue D'Espagne.' He glanced at Eve. 'I said it right, didn't I?' She nodded and he went on, 'Evan is going to meet us there.'

'Oh, is he?' Dean said curtly, the smile vanishing from his face. 'Enjoy yourselves. I will see you this evening.'

Eve felt rather flat after he had gone. She cleared the dishes, took them to the kitchen, and then told Tommy to collect his school books.

'Do we have to have lessons today?' he grumbled.

'Yes. You know we do. It will only be for an hour.'

Hearing loud bangs and thumps coming from the roof, she guessed that Samira was banging the mats up there. 'We shall have to sit out on the patio today,' she told Tommy before he went up the stairs to fetch his books.

Eve arranged the table and chairs to her liking after she had pulled them into the shade, then sat down and waited. Tommy joined her, looking very reluctant, and the lesson commenced. Samira made a great deal of noise bringing the rugs down from the roof and for a few minutes Eve could not hear herself speak. Then the kitchen door closed and silence prevailed.

Half an hour passed, then the doorbell rang. Thinking that it could only be Evan, Eve hurried through the living-room and met Samira in the hall.

'I will answer it, Samira,' she said. 'I expect it's Mr Morgan.'

But when Eve threw open the door it was not Evan standing there but an attractive woman in a navy blue dress with white trimmings. She had two cases either side of her and a large handbag slung over one shoulder.

'Could I see Mr Rimmer?' she asked quietly.

'I'm sorry. You have missed him. He went out about an hour ago.'

'It doesn't really matter. I can see him later. Do you think I could come in?'

Eve hesitated. 'Mr Rimmer won't be back until this evening.'

'That's okay. Would you give me a hand with these cases? Be careful of that one. It has some valuable instruments in it.'

Feeling at a loss, Eve did as the woman suggested. Samira was standing in the hall looking at them suspiciously, and, recalling Dean's warning, Eve spoke to her sharply.

'I'm sure you have things to do, Samira!'

The Arab woman's dark eyes glinted with anger, but she left them without saying anything, and Eve took the visitor into the living-room and shut the door.

'You look rather exhausted,' she said kindly. 'Would you care for a drink or something to eat?'

'No, thanks. I had breakfast in town. Sorry to startle you like this. I'm Doctor Nadia Green. I guess you are Tommy's governess.'

Eve looked surprised. 'You know

about Tommy? I came with him from England. I'm staying with him until he has settled down. I've been here two months. I expect I shall be leaving in a week or two.'

'Dean hasn't mentioned me?'

'No.'

Nadia nodded, then smiled at the boy, who had come in to see what was happening. 'You are tall, Tommy! Don't be scared. You and I are going to get along fine, aren't we?'

Eve quickly took the opportunity to study the woman. So far she had been impressed by her manner and good looks. She had light brown hair, naturally wavy, Eve guessed, brown eyes and a lovely, clear skin evenly sun-tanned. She was about twenty-six, Eve thought, as she eyed the woman's slim figure and admired the elegant way in which she stood. She's used to telling people what to do and she commands respect, Eve decided. She was extremely puzzled by the sudden arrival of the doctor and if she had not sensed a kindred spirit, might have treated her in a more cautious way.

Tommy said plaintively, 'Do I have to do my lessons, Eve?'

She smiled. 'No. You can pack up now.'

'Eve?' Nadia remarked. 'That's an unusual name nowadays. It suits you.' Her eyes twinkled. 'It's too bad of me arriving suddenly and surprising you. But Dean and I are old friends. He would have wanted me to come here.'

Eve frowned. 'You are going to stay?'

'Yes. I shall have to.'

'Have you been here before?' Eve broke off, then said apologetically, 'Forgive me. It's nothing to do with me.'

'That's okay. I don't mind. I would be curious also. I've never seen this house. Dean told me about it. I'm not a frequent visitor to Tangier. I've spent the last two years in the border towns between Algeria and Morocco.'

'You aren't attached to any hospital?'

'Not now. I used to be. Then when I

discovered that some towns never saw a doctor or nurse I attempted to fill the gap.'

'It sounds a brave thing to do. There are so many nationalities. Are the tribesmen friendly?'

'Fairly. I've had some opposition from primitive tribes where they prefer to rely on their magic healers. But Arabs and Berbers are courteous people. I guess some of them thought I was crazy.'

'Do you travel alone?'

'No. Mohamed, an old Arab, used to accompany me. He was very useful because he knew so many dialects and he drove the estate car for me. Also I could rely on him to find suitable quarters for me, and by that I mean fairly clean ones.'

'Was that difficult?'

Nadia chuckled. 'Sometimes I thought I was wasted as a doctor. I spent most of my time teaching basic hygiene.' She became serious as she went on thoughtfully, 'When I first came out here I was horrified with the plight of the women. I've become more accustomed to it now, but not resigned. Often the girls are married at twelve and have a baby every year. Added to that they are expected to do all the menial tasks. They work in the fields, carry water and heavy loads, prepare food and do all the normal tasks a housewife is supposed to do.'

'Is that typical throughout Morocco?'

'Not in the cities. But I spent most of my time in the desert, where I frequently encountered these young women. Imagine living in tents and enduring a life like that!'

'Do you change anything by visiting these nomad tribes?'

Nadia smiled ruefully. 'Not much. Occasionally I saved a baby or a woman's life. I'm a gynaecologist, so I didn't find that difficult. No, I guess the answer lies in schooling. To alter anything one has to start with the youngsters.'

Tommy had been running about the room, darting out to the patio at intervals. Now he had tired himself out he went up to Eve and clung to her, resting his head against her side.

'Can't we go to the sea?' he asked disconsolately.

'Had you planned to go out?' Nadia exclaimed.

'I had promised to meet someone on the beach.'

'Don't let me stop you,' Nadia said considerately. 'Is there a room I could use? I would like to unpack some of my things.'

'There are only three bedrooms. Samira sleeps in and Tommy and I share one. Mr Rimmer has the other. He did offer to move into his den when I came. That's a small room behind this one.'

'I can use that one, then. Is there anything I can sleep on?'

'There's a single bed which folds up. I will ask Samira to bring you the linen and blankets.'

'Is she the woman I saw when I arrived?'

'Yes. She's the housekeeper.' Eve walked across to the door and opened it. She glanced out at the empty hall, then went back to Nadia, who was looking at her curiously. 'She's very inquisitive, so be careful what you say to her.'

Nadia nodded. 'I've learned to be discreet. Will you be back for lunch?'

Eve noticed that Tommy was gazing at her anxiously. She gave him a comforting smile before she replied. 'We had planned to eat out. Evan, he's a local school-master, usually takes us to various restaurants when he can spare the time. Why don't you come with us?'

The doctor seemed doubtful. 'I guess not. It's important that I see Dean before I venture out.'

'Samira will be going out this morning. She won't return until late this afternoon. But there's sure to be something in the refrigerator.'

'Don't worry about me. I can make myself at home anywhere. You and

Tommy go out and enjoy yourselves.'

Eve went in search of Samira and was surprised to find her cleaning out the den. Had she overheard their conversation or was it coincidence Eve wondered?

'Doctor Green is going to stay with us for a few days,' Eve said after the woman had switched off the vacuum cleaner. 'Would you make the bed up in here?'

'Was Mr Rimmer expecting her?' Samira's dark eyes were boldly inquisitive.

'That's no concern of ours, Samira. Please make her as comfortable as you can.'

'I had made plans for this afternoon.' She hesitated, then added, 'I was going out this morning, too. You said you would be out.'

'Yes. I've told Doctor Green that you are going. She will get her own lunch.'

Samira nodded. Eve was disturbed by the unconcealed excitement emanating from the woman, for there was no mistaking the smile of triumph on the brown face or the malicious glint in the black eyes. Because she felt uneasy, Eve said nothing more and went thoughtfully back to the living-room to collect Tommy.

4

The outing with Evan was not a success. Eve was quiet, too preoccupied with her troubled thoughts to take much notice of her companion. He had arranged to take them sightseeing after lunch and was disappointed at her lack of interest.

'What's the matter, Eve?' he asked as they came out of one of the museums and began to thread their way back across the Medina. 'You've hardly said a word all day.'

'Surely I haven't been as quiet as that!' she protested mildly. She felt tempted to mention the arrival of Doctor Green, but prudence kept her silent. If Tommy had said something she would have had to explain, but the boy had been too interested in the day's activities to remember. 'I feel rather tired today. It's hotter than usual, isn't it?'

Evan's face brightened. 'Yes, it is. You're not used to this dry heat. If that's all it is I'm sorry I spoke. I thought I might have upset you.'

'No. I've enjoyed your company. It was good of you to take so much trouble.'

He said seriously, 'I would do anything for you, Eve. You know that, don't you?'

Eve stared at him in surprise, carefully hiding her dismay at his ardent expression. Luckily she was saved from replying for a group of Arab boys suddenly parted them. And when she rejoined Evan she carefully spoke of something else. He looked downcast, for he had been longing to find out if she felt as he did. But he was very sensitive and sensed her reluctance, so decided to leave it for another day. Eve was worth waiting for and he did not want to frighten her off by rushing things.

Unaware of the depth of Evan's feelings, Eve chatted to him in her usual manner, and when Evan saw them on to the bus which would take them to the end of their avenue, she promptly forgot all about him. Her mind was too full of the sudden arrival of Nadia and she was wondering what Dean's reaction was going to be when he came home that evening.

As it happened, Dean returned to the house just after four o'clock. He guessed that Eve might be there and was looking forward to having tea with her and Tommy. Opening the front door, he caught a whiff of Turkish tobacco and immediately became aware that a visitor had arrived. He moved to the open doorway and paused there to eye the young woman who was lying on the settee with her head in a nest of pillows.

'Doctor Nadia, I presume!' he drawled, and grinned when she started in alarm and opened her eyes.

'I didn't hear you come in.' She smiled, but did not attempt to get up. 'I've taken my shoes off. I won't get up.'

Dean moved closer, taking a chair near her. 'I didn't expect you for a couple of weeks.'

'I know. I'm sorry about that. Things were becoming too hot for me. I had to leave Fez in a hurry. In fact I got out so quickly that I left some of my things behind.'

'What happened?' Dean asked, looking at her anxiously. 'Did something scare you?'

'I guess so.' She smiled faintly. 'The first incident could have been an accident. I thought so at the time. Mohamed and I were rammed by a truck miles from anywhere. We survived that. Then a few days later, when we were back in our quarters — we were staying just outside Fez at the time — someone tried to poison me. Mohamed and I sat down to eat together, but I got up to fetch some aspirin because I had a headache. When I went back I found my Arab friend writhing in agony. I was still working on him three hours later.' Her voice broke and tears sprang to her brown eyes. 'I couldn't save him. He died later that night.'

Dean's face had become taut and pale. He leaned over and pressed his fingers over her hand. 'I'm real sorry. I guess you were fond of him.'

She sniffed and brushed the tears away. 'I had known him a long time. He was a loyal old man.'

'What did you do then?'

'I carried on; found another driver. But I had become suspicious and was much more wary. Then one evening as we were driving back from Sefrou, someone fired a bullet through the side window of the estate wagon. I had left my bag on the back seat and I chose that moment to lean right back to get it. If I had been sitting where I had been a second before I would have been hit in the head. The bullet tore a strip off my driver's back. The car skidded and we landed up against the side of a hill.' Nadia shrugged her slim shoulders and smiled twistedly. 'I got the message.

Three times was enough. Evidently the enemy is determined to get me. When I got back to Fez I packed a few things and left that night. I drove to Sidi Kacem, dumped the car, and came the rest of the way by train.'

Dean was frowning and he looked worried. 'This alters our plans, doesn't it?'

'I guess so.' Nadia blew smoke into the air, then went on seriously, 'I can't stay here too long. Luckily the three months is nearly up. It's obvious that they have discovered I know something. But they don't know that I have already passed on the information. They wouldn't be so desperate to get rid of me if they had guessed that.'

'Do you think you were followed?'

'I doubt it. I acted so swiftly.'

Dean said grimly, 'They will soon be informed. My housekeeper will tell them you have arrived.'

'Samira?' Nadia's fine eyebrows rose in surprise. 'Is she in their pay?'

'I'm pretty sure.'

'Eve told me to be careful.'

Dean said quickly, 'You've met her?'

'Yes. She let me in.' Nadia's brown eyes twinkled. 'I didn't expect to see such a young woman. She's real pretty.'

Dean frowned. 'That was Anita's doing. I asked her to send someone capable.'

'Eve seems sensible enough.'

'She is, but I would have preferred an older woman.'

'I guess Eve would be sympathetic. Why don't you explain the difficulty we're in?'

'I've been tempted, but it would be too dangerous. I know she's guessed that something is wrong, but the less she knows the safer she will be.' Dean eyed Nadia thoughtfully. 'We shall have to give Samira a good reason for you being here. They will expect us to move out and will be puzzled when we don't go.'

Nadia nodded. 'It's a pity I had to come too early. My arrival is going to focus attention on this house. I've made it more dangerous for you.'

'I'm not too worried. That was the idea, wasn't it, to keep your enemies pinned down. It's Eve I'm concerned about. I wish I could send her back.'

'If things had gone as planned you could have done that in a couple of weeks. Now we shall have to have someone to look after Tommy. Would she be able to cope on her own?'

'That's okay. I've spoken to her about that.'

'Wasn't she curious?'

'If she was she was too polite to ask questions. I had told her I couldn't explain. It's rather like sitting on a keg of gunpowder with Samira watching and listening all the time. It's a relief to know she's out right now.'

'I've thought of what we can say to her,' Nadia exclaimed, and smiled in a satisfied way. 'It's very simple. We will tell her the truth. Marriage, that's why I've come. The wedding is going to be earlier than arranged.'

Dean was silent for so long that she

110

glanced at him curiously. 'Why the dark frown? Can you think of a better excuse?'

'No.'

'It will seem logical. I told several people in Fez that I was going to marry Dean Rimmer. That was a few weeks ago. The news will have leaked through by now.'

'Yes.' Dean spoke reluctantly. 'We shall have to make it plain that that is why you have come. It will give me time to make arrangements to have you smuggled out of Tangier. Ali-ben-Ahmed has a boat. I'm pretty certain that he will help us, but I shall have to tread warily. It may take a few days.'

'It means saying goodbye to all this,' Nadia remarked with a careless wave of her hand at the room.

'We can't take anything,' Dean replied firmly. 'Material possessions can be replaced. There's too much at stake to worry about trifles.' He lifted his head and listened. 'That's Samira now. She's returned to cook the dinner.'

'You could get rid of her. Tell her I'm going to run the house.'

'Don't be silly! That would look suspicious. If she asks I shall say we would like her to stay on because you are going to work at the hospital in Tangier. That will give the impression that we intend to stay.'

'Okay. I can drop a few hints.'

Dean nodded. 'Keep all remarks trivial from now on. I never know when she's listening.'

Eve came in a few minutes later with Tommy and, as she went up the stairs to the bathroom, intending to supervise his nightly bath, she noticed that the door of the den was open. Nadia came out and waved up at her.

'Sorry about the noise.' She smiled and moved to the foot of the stairs. 'Are you coming down again, Tommy?'

'Yes. I can have my supper in my dressing-gown.'

'That's good. I want to talk to you.'

Eve left Tommy to amuse himself in the bath and went down to lay a place for him on a corner of the dining table. Then she went to the kitchen to dish up whatever was ready. She preferred to do this herself because Samira grumbled if she had to interrupt her cooking to see to Tommy. Eve usually managed to find something for the boy and if nothing was ready would open a small tin of meat and prepare a salad. Tommy always had a good mid-day meal so a light meal at night suited him best. She had become used to his likes and dislikes, so she did not have to give his food a great deal of thought or stay too long in the kitchen.

As Tommy usually left pools of water in the bathroom if he was left to himself, Eve dashed upstairs to clean up and empty the water. Then, with Tommy looking young and guileless with his dampened hair and rosy cheeks poking up over his fluffy dressing-gown, Eve ushered him into the living-room.

'What is it?' he asked, skipping around her when she came in with his supper.

'Stewed steak tonight. Samira put it in the oven before she went out.'

'Good, I like that!'

Nadia had heard them come down and came in to join them. 'Would you like me to read to you?' she asked Tommy as he began to eat.

He nodded his fair head. 'Is it science fiction?'

Nadia raised her eyebrows at Eve. 'I guess I've never indulged in those. Is there any particular one you prefer?'

Eve smiled. 'Dean has a few. I started reading one to Tommy soon after we arrived because I couldn't find anything suitable. We've nearly finished it. Shall I get it for you?'

'No. I don't want to spoil your routine. When do you read to him?'

'When he's tucked up in bed. He's asleep after a couple of pages.'

Nadia sat down at the table. 'A talk will do just as well. What do you think of Tangier, Tommy?'

He was paying little attention for he was eyeing the ice-cream and fruit salad

Eve had put on the table. 'You said I wasn't to have that at night,' he said doubtfully.

'There was nothing else. Once won't hurt you. It's only a small portion.'

Nadia tried again. Trying to focus Tommy's attention on herself was more difficult than she had imagined. But she had to let the news leak out somehow and she did not want Tommy to hear it from someone else. It might upset him.

'Do you miss your home in England?' she asked tentatively.

As she spoke Dean came in from the patio and closed the french windows. He had gone out there to consider what he ought to do and had ignored the fading light. He drew the curtains across and sat down in an armchair near the dining table.

'I wish Auntie was here.' Tommy gulped a mouthful of ice-cream too quickly, making tears spring to his eyes.

'Take smaller spoonfuls,' Eve said kindly.

'Yes, I guess you do miss her, but you enjoy seeing new places?' Nadia asked, giving him an indulgent smile.

He nodded. 'I think 'Mocco' is great.'

'Do you like meeting new people?'

'Yes, if they are funny.' He gave a delicious giggle.

Nadia pulled a face. 'I'm a disappointment then.'

Tommy gazed at her curiously. 'Why?'

'I'm just an ordinary person.'

Eve said quickly, 'I wouldn't say that, Nadia. You are braver than most women.' She turned to Tommy, who was looking at them solemnly. 'She actually goes into the desert and lives with the nomad tribes. You've been told about them, Tommy, haven't you?'

'Did you see lots of camels?' he asked eagerly.

'Sure.' Nadia smiled at Eve, grateful because she was making her task easier. 'Now I've left all that. I've come to stay with you and Daddy.'

'For always?'

'I guess so. We aren't going to leave you on your own again. Your Daddy and I are going to look after you. We are going to be a real family.'

Eve guessed where this conversation was leading and tried desperately to hide her dismay. Yet at the same time she felt compelled to help Tommy grasp what Nadia was explaining to him and to accept without resentment.

'You will be as fortunate as all your friends at school,' she told him gently. 'You will have a Mummy and a Daddy to look after you.'

Hurt because Tommy was looking so bewildered, Nadia put her arm around him and said in a low voice, 'It won't be too difficult, Tommy. We like each other already, don't we?'

'You will be my Mummy?' Tommy asked doubtfully.

Eve flicked a glance at Dean, then quickly looked away. He was sitting on the edge of his chair listening to them, his face taut and inscrutable. Eve wondered why he was not helping

Nadia to explain to Tommy. The boy might have accepted it more easily from him. It's strange how aloof Dean is with his son, she thought. It's almost as if he's scared to allow the boy to become fond of him.

'Sure, honey,' Nadia was saying. 'Your Daddy and I are going to get married real soon. That's why I gave up my work in the desert. I wanted to come and look after you both.'

'Will I have Eve as well?'

'For a little while.' Nadia hesitated, then said gently, 'Eve has her own home to go back to. But I'm sure she will write to you.'

Tommy blinked and two tears rolled down his cheeks. 'I don't want Eve to go,' he mumbled.

Eve stood up, wiped his tears away and put her arm across his shoulders. 'I'm not going this very minute, silly. Come on! I will take you up to bed. And tomorrow if you are good we can go and see the snake charmer. You would like that, wouldn't you?'

Tommy's eyes lit up. 'The conjurer as well?'

'That's enough,' Eve said firmly. 'We won't have time to see everything. But the snake charmer I do promise you shall see.'

When Eve and Tommy had gone, Nadia sighed aloud. She seemed troubled as she took a chair close to Dean.

'That was frightful! I ought not to have broken it like that. But what else could I have done? It would have been easier to talk about it to Eve when Samira was hovering about, so that she would have got the message, but I didn't think it would be fair to Tommy to hear it casually. Children are so sensitive and it's important to me that Tommy isn't resentful.'

'He's too young to feel that,' Dean said quietly. 'Now you have told him he will begin to accept. Eve helped. The boy is fond of her and will take notice of what she says.'

'She is an understanding young

woman. I sensed that she was not happy about it. I guess it was a shock for her also. But she hid her embarrassment and came to my aid. I'm real grateful and will tell her so later on.'

'Eve considers others first, just as you do, Nadia.' Dean smiled. 'When Tommy wakes tomorrow it will be no longer new. He will take it for granted and begin to confide in you. Cheer up, Nadia! Don't look so gloomy.'

Nadia frowned as she glanced at him. 'Suddenly, I feel frightened. That's strange because for the last two years fear has never bothered me. Now everything seems different.'

'It's because happiness is within your grasp. You are scared something might happen to take it away.'

'Yes, you're right. The next few days seem fraught with danger.'

'It won't be if we remain calm. Don't panic and don't say much whilst you remain in this house. Speak and act naturally. Your future is in my hands now.'

Dinner that evening was a painful ordeal for Eve. Finding it difficult to converse with Dean, she remained silent unless she was spoken to. Nadia did not notice for she was enjoying telling Dean about the life she had been leading. Once or twice Dean tried to draw Eve into the conversation, but did not persist when he saw how ill at ease she looked.

Eve took the dishes out to Samira and returned with the coffee. Nadia and Dean were sitting close together, talking in low voices, but stopped when Eve walked across to them.

'I ought to have helped you,' Nadia remarked with a smile at Eve.

'I expect you are tired. Anyway, there's no need. I don't have very much to do.' She served them with the coffee, then sat down to drink hers.

'Did Tommy say anything about our talk before he went to sleep?' Nadia asked curiously.

'No. I didn't expect him to. He will think about it quietly to himself. He's a reserved child and it's kinder not to rush him. I think you will find that he's excited and pleased, but he won't tell you that. He will be very cautious for a day or two. He has always known that he was different to his friends. He used to ask why he hadn't a Mummy and Daddy at home. Anita was very kind to him, but it wasn't the same. I expect that's why he keeps things to himself more than other children do.'

Nadia nodded her head. 'You understand youngsters, Eve. It's a gift, I guess.'

Eve smiled faintly. 'No. It's my job to deal with them intelligently. I think it's important for a teacher to know as much as she can about the background of each individual child.'

'That's a lot to expect from any teacher,' Dean remarked.

'It depends on the size of each class. Most teachers do their best. I was lucky. I had only twenty infants to look after and I saw their mothers nearly every day.'

'I can see what you mean about Tommy. He never had a parent to show off to his friends.'

'That's right. His aunt loved him, but it's never the same. Children need to love someone who belongs. They need security above all else. Anita always knew that one day she might have to part with Tommy, so she tried to make him self-reliant. For a child of his age it was not easy.'

'He will have security from now on,' Nadia said firmly. 'I shall make it up to him. I had expected a certain amount of opposition and was surprised that he took it so well.'

'He doesn't remember his mother, so that made it easier,' Eve said thoughtfully. 'You aren't taking anyone's place.'

'Only yours,' Nadia smiled. 'He's real attached to you, Eve.'

'That's because he has to rely on me and I'm part of his environment back home. He will soon forget me.'

'I hope not,' Dean said. 'None of us will ever forget you, Eve.'

Nadia drank the remains of her coffee and stood up. 'I'm going to have a bath and turn in. It's been a long day and I'm feeling terribly sleepy. I can take the cups back to the kitchen on my way.'

After she had gone Eve said quietly, 'I might as well have an early night too.'

Dean spoke quickly, 'Don't go for a minute. I want to thank you for helping Nadia.'

Eve smiled faintly. 'It was nothing. I was afraid Tommy might have been upset. It was to make it easier for him.'

'You succeeded very well. Eve, for Pete's sake don't look so . . . hurt!'

She bit her bottom lip and turned her face away from his keen eyes. 'I didn't know I was,' she said, striving to keep her voice steady. 'I expect it was the surprise I got. You had not mentioned Nadia or your intentions.'

'I wanted to tell you,' he said gruffly.

'I wish you had said something. I thought we were friends, not just employer and child companion.' She broke off, aware that she was in danger of revealing how upset she was.

'We were more than that, Eve.' Dean sounded ill at ease. 'I hate hurting you like this. I wish I could explain. It's not easy for me either. I want you to know that.'

'How can you say that?' There was a hint of bitterness in her voice. 'You were expecting Nadia to come here?'

'Yes, but not for a couple of weeks.'

'Then perhaps I'm lucky,' Eve said shakily. 'You knew you were going to marry her.'

There was a few minutes of silence. If Eve had looked at Dean she would have been concerned to see how pale and harassed he appeared. But she was too caught up in her own distress to notice.

'A marriage was arranged,' he said expressionlessly.

'Nadia's extremely suitable. Tommy likes her.'

'Yes.' Dean frowned, glanced at Eve's set face and looked away.

Eve said quietly, 'There seems no

need for me to stay any longer, Mr Rimmer. It might be better for Nadia and Tommy if I went. Tommy will soon become used to Nadia.'

Dean moved abruptly, swinging round so that he could face her. 'I understand your desire to go, Eve, and I have no right to ask you to stay. But have you forgotten that conversation we had soon after you arrived? The situation is still the same. I'm depending on you to keep Tommy safe.'

She looked puzzled. 'Surely, Nadia will do that?'

He shook his head. 'I didn't want to tell you this, but I can see that I shall have to now.' He lowered his voice to almost a whisper. 'The reason why Nadia came here earlier than expected was because there have been three attempts on her life.'

'Oh, how awful!' Eve gasped.

'It's complicated matters. One day I shall be able to explain it all to you, Eve, but it's safer if you know nothing. What I do want you to understand is that only you can look after Tommy. Circumstances could arise where Nadia and I would be helpless to keep him safe.'

'Then it's important that I do stay,' Eve said quietly. 'My feelings don't come into this. I can see that now. Tommy's safety must come first.'

Dean smiled. 'Thanks, Eve. I knew you wouldn't let me down.' Involuntarily he put his hand on her shoulder and pressed into her flesh, unconscious of his strength. She flinched and drew away, her face losing most of its colour.

Dean watched her, his blue eyes revealing the depth of his longing and frustration. Had Eve noticed, she would have been bewildered and curious, but she was gazing away from him, fighting the emotion which entangled her.

With a tremendous effort she said steadily, 'Nadia will have finished in the bathroom. Good night, Dean,' and left the room swiftly before he could reply.

Dean remained where he was for a few minutes with a dark scowl on his face. Then, moving across to the bookcase, he took out a large-scale map of the Moroccan coastline and spread it over the table. As he concentrated his scowl disappeared and his eyes became acutely keen and observant.

He heard Nadia run down the stairs and go to the den, then waited patiently for Samira to retire before he turned out the light and left the dining-room. He looked very thoughtful as he climbed the stairs to his room. The interview with Eve had been more exhausting than he had realised, for suddenly he felt weary of the entire set-up. Yet he knew that he could not turn back now. He had to go on. All their lives depended on his tenacity and cunning.

5

Dean had been right about Tommy. The next morning the boy chatted incessantly to Eve as she dressed him, asking questions about the new life he was going to lead. As he did not wait for her to reply, Eve merely listened and smiled, giving him a nod of her head occasionally. The child was bubbling over with excitement and Eve thought it wiser to allow him to talk without interruption. She was only too thankful that he had accepted so readily the changes which were in store for him. She had feared tears and fits of temper.

Silently she thanked Anita, who had prepared the boy for such an eventuality. It could not have been easy for her, Eve thought. I know she loved Tommy very much. It would have been painful to hide her motherly instincts so that the boy would not rely on her too much. I wish Dean was more grateful for what she has done. He has taken it all without a word of praise. But perhaps I'm being too critical. Only a woman could understand how Anita felt.

With childish candour Tommy informed Samira that he was going to have a real Mummy. That he spoke to the woman without any hesitation showed that he was thrilled with the prospect, for normally he avoided Samira because he was frightened of her. But that morning he was so full of his important news he forgot his fear.

'Nadia has come here 'specially to look after me,' he said proudly. 'We are going to make a family.'

Samira put down the saucepan she had been scouring and turned to look at him. Her penetrating black eyes were sharp but her thick, flat features revealed no surprise as she questioned him.

'Does that mean you are going away?'

'No, silly!' Tommy giggled. 'Nadia is

going to live with Daddy and me in this house.'

'I don't believe you. You are making it up.'

'I'm not!' the boy cried shrilly, jumping up and down with indignation. 'Nadia is going to be 'mawied'.' He could never sound his 'r's' when he was excited.

Samira grunted disbelievingly, 'Your Daddy is going to marry Doctor Green?'

'Yes. I just told you! Isn't it 'citing?'

Samira patted him on the head. 'You be good boy now and find Miss Lovell. I have to go out soon.'

Tommy ran off and found Eve and Nadia in the living-room. Dean had gone to his office as usual.

'Samira was 'stounded!' he said, swaggering with pride as he confronted Eve.

Nadia glanced at him curiously. 'You have told her I'm going to marry your Daddy?'

'Yes, but she wasn't very interested.'

He pouted. 'She never listens to me. She always has to go out.'

Eve said quickly, 'Did she say that just now?'

'Yes. I'm not going to tell her anything else, however important.'

He looked so downcast that Eve knelt down and hugged him. 'Never mind, Tommy. I'm excited. I think you are very lucky and you're going to be so happy.'

Nadia was smiling broadly. 'I got the message across then. That's a relief.'

Eve glanced up at her curiously. Then she stood up, keeping her hand on Tommy's shoulder. 'You wanted Samira to know?'

'Yes. I was hoping Tommy would tell her. I had to give her a good reason for my being here.'

Eve's heart lurched hopefully, but she spoke cautiously. 'There's no truth in it, then? Was it just an excuse?'

'No, it's true enough,' Nadia said carelessly. 'Dean asked me to marry him about six months ago. I've known him for two years. That is why I came here.'

'I suppose you are relieved that you can be together now,' Eve said awkwardly. 'He told me what happened to you.'

'He did?' Nadia stared at her in surprise.

Tommy had run out to the patio, so Eve had no qualms about explaining. 'I thought I wouldn't be needed now that you have come. Dean had to explain why he still wanted me here.'

'Yes.' Nadia stared at her thoughtfully. 'I expect it is difficult for you, Eve. I'm used to looking over my shoulder to see if I'm being followed. Dean and I have agreed that it is safer for you not to know what we are involved in. And we shall breathe more easily if we can rely on you to care for Tommy. It won't be for long.' She hesitated, then added, 'I guess you know that Samira spies on us?'

'Yes. Dean told me some time ago.'

Nadia nodded. 'He would have had

to warn you about her. She listens to all our conversations and reports any items of news.' She laughed mirthlessly. 'How thankful I shall be when it's all over and we can lead normal lives again! The strain has been almost too much.'

'I can imagine.' Eve smiled sympathetically. 'I will do anything I can to help.'

'Bless you.' Nadia put her arm around Eve's waist and gave her a gentle hug. 'It's real nice having you around. We were lucky that Anita chose you.'

'How did you come to meet Dean?' Eve asked curiously. 'I've guessed that you are an American. Did you meet him before you came over here?'

'No.' Nadia smiled. 'I guess I can tell you that. I told you I used to tour round the desert camps, didn't I? Occasionally I would return to my headquarters in Fez so that I could pick up my mail and get a fresh stock of medical supplies. It was on one of those trips that I ran into Dean. After that we met often, but because of our commitments couldn't allow our relationship to become serious. Then quite suddenly a few weeks ago something happened which altered both our lives. I was unable to continue working in the desert and Dean asked me to come to Tangier to be with him.'

'Have you decided where you will live?'

Nadia shook her head. 'Don't ask me any more, Eve. I feel it's tempting providence. I wouldn't have said all this now, but I feel a mite reckless with Samira out of the house. I guess it's not fair to you, but underneath my anxiety I'm excited and happy. I've waited for so long to share Dean's life with him. But it wasn't possible and I had to be patient. And even now I have to keep a rein on my thoughts. We are not out of the woods yet and a slip of the tongue could ruin any chance of happiness for Dean and myself. It's so easy to disappear in this country.'

'When do you plan to get married?'

'In a month's time, I hope. That's for your ears only, Eve. I want Samira to believe it's going to be sooner.'

Eve looked puzzled. 'Would it make a difference if she did know?' She smiled. 'I suppose that's another thing I'm to remain in the dark about.'

'Yes. I've said too much already.' Nadia began to walk to the door. She paused and looked back. 'Is Evan calling for you this morning?'

'No. He has to teach today. I promised Tommy I would take him to the Medina.'

'I remember. I might as well come with you. I don't fancy staying in alone today.'

'Ought you to go out? Will it be safe?'

Nadia laughed. 'As safe as anywhere. Plans may be afoot to eliminate me, but I guess they won't strike yet. I guess they are a wee bit puzzled, and that's how I want them to be. They will wait to see if we make a move. If we act normally it will quieten their suspicions.'

'I hope so,' Eve said uneasily. 'How can you be so calm?'

'What is to be, will be. I'm a firm believer in Kismet. I've had three lucky escapes. I'm scared, Eve. I'm not as brave as I appear to be. But I'm happier than I've been for months. Safety is not far off now. And I guess Dean and I will be happier than most couples who have not had to wait.'

Nadia, Eve and Tommy had not returned by the time Dean came home that evening, and he spent a few anxious minutes wondering whether they were all right. His anxiety was so acute that he was impervious to Samira's surprised expression when he asked her if she knew where they had gone.

'I was not here when they went out,' the woman said. 'You are afraid for them?'

Dean frowned. 'No, certainly not. It seems strange that they are not in, that's all.'

'Women can walk safely in Tangier

now. It is not as it used to be.' Samira gave him a sly glance. 'What would you do if they did not come back?'

'Inform the police.' Dean stared at her, suddenly alert. 'What are you hinting at, Samira?'

'Nothing . . . I know nothing,' the woman mumbled.

Dean ignored her and went into the living-room. He felt too on edge to sit down and took refuge in the patio where he paced up and down. And when he heard a car draw up and the excited clamour of Tommy's high-pitched voice, he could contain himself no longer. He pushed through the bushes on to the path and confronted all three as they were approaching the house.

'Where the heck have you been!' he exclaimed angrily. 'Eve, do you know what time it is?'

Eve glanced at him in surprise. 'We went to the beach this morning and then looked round the shops. Nadia wanted to buy a few things.'

'Another time leave a note where you intend going,' Dean said curtly. 'I've been anxious. You are usually in by five o'clock.'

'I'm sorry.' Eve flicked a glance at Nadia, who was looking amused. 'I didn't think you would mind if we kept Tommy out.'

'I don't in the sense you mean.' Dean ran his fingers through his hair awkwardly. His face was less pale and disturbed and he managed a faint smile.

'Tommy was perfectly safe. I kept an eye on him all the time.'

Nadia said dryly, 'I guess it wasn't Tommy he was worried about.'

Dean gave her an annoyed glance and said stiffly, 'I was anxious about you all.'

Tommy pushed his way forward. 'See what Nadia bought me!' he cried excitedly, holding up a model of a camel for Dean to see. 'It moves its legs. Can I show you?'

'Another time, Tommy,' Dean replied

abruptly. 'Samira has dinner ready.'

Feeling sorry for Tommy, Eve said quickly, 'Come along. You can have dinner with us tonight and have your bath afterwards.'

Dean waited until Eve and Tommy had gone inside, then turned on Nadia, who was taking her time, sauntering along with an armful of parcels. 'You ought not to have gone out, Nadia. Here, let me give you a hand with those!'

'I guess not. I shall drop them.'

'What in heavens name made you buy anything?' he said irritably. 'You know you can't take them with you.'

'I say, you are agitated.' Nadia was looking astonished. 'What's happened?'

'Nothing. I was anxious because Eve and Tommy didn't come in at their usual time. It's natural to feel annoyed afterwards.'

'I notice you weren't concerned about me!' Nadia laughed.

'It's different for you, Nadia. You are used to looking after yourself.'

'Thanks!' She smiled wryly.

'I thought I heard a car. Didn't you come back by bus?'

'We bumped into Evan in town and he offered to drive us back. He's a nice young man. Did you know he's in love with Eve?'

'Yes.'

Nadia smiled at his scowling face. 'So that's why you are so grumpy! I'm sorry, honey. Things are real complicated, aren't they?'

Dean shrugged his shoulders. 'They needn't be if we keep our heads.'

'I guess you are finding that difficult. We ought to go in. Samira will imagine we're hatching some plot or other.'

Eve was thankful for Tommy's presence at dinner that evening. He kept her occupied and prevented her from saying much to Nadia and Dean. Tommy was pleased that he was being allowed to stay up, but Eve was still smarting from the way Dean had lashed out at her; unfairly, she thought. It hurt also to know that he cared for Nadia's safety so much that he could get into a panic when she was absent for a few hours. Eve did not think that he had been worried about Tommy. He would know that Eve would look after him.

Tommy gave Eve a good excuse to retire early, which was just as well, for she did not feel in the mood to sit with Dean and Nadia whilst they drank coffee. They would have many things to talk over and she hated feeling in the way. So when Tommy had finished his dessert she remarked casually:

'I won't bother to come down again. I will stay with Tommy and read to him.'

Nadia nodded and smiled. 'Thanks for the lovely day, Eve.'

Dean said nothing. Eve glanced at him, noticed his stern, preoccupied expression, and decided to follow Tommy from the room without saying anything else.

'You might have said something,' Nadia drawled reproachfully. 'Eve is too nice to ignore.'

'What did you want me to say?' Dean scowled.

'An apology wouldn't have come amiss.'

'What for?'

Nadia smiled. 'Eve's a sensitive person. You were curt with her.'

'For Pete's sake, don't go on about it! Surely I'm permitted to be bad-tempered occasionally?'

'Sure, why not?' Nadia said equably. 'I will take the coffee cups back and see where Samira is at the same time.'

She returned a few minutes later looking well satisfied. 'She's gone to her room. I noticed the light was on.'

'That's a relief.' Dean leaned back in his chair and smiled at her apologetically. 'I've had a hectic day.'

'I guessed you had. Did you contact your friend?'

'Yes. It was complicated. I didn't want to go to his house openly. As you know, I'm watched closely all day.'

'How did you see him, then?'

'I gave it a great deal of thought

before I remembered the guy who has an office beneath mine. Luckily we became acquainted some time ago, so it didn't seem odd when I asked him to do me a favour. He's an American like me and gets a bit homesick sometimes. Believe it or not, he's an agent for a wallpaper firm. Not that he sells much of that, but he tells me he gets big contracts for paints, brushes and so on. Some have been government contracts.'

'Can you trust him?'

'Sure. Bill Freeman's discreet. He's been in Morocco some years. I dropped into his office this morning and told him I wanted to get in touch with the merchant, Ali-ben-Ahmed. He understood without any explanation that I didn't want to draw attention to myself. He offered to contact Ali and arrange for us to meet in his office.'

'Did Ali turn up?'

'Yes, this afternoon. To allay suspicion Ali placed an order with Bill, an authentic one, much to our delight. Bill rang me up to tell me and I took it as a signal to go down to his office. I slipped out without being seen.'

'Did you explain to Ali about me?'

'I didn't have to. He knows far more than I had suspected. He knew you were in Tangier and guessed you were in trouble. It beats me how he keeps in contact with people behind the scenes. He's moderate in his outlook. This country needs guys like him. He puts his country first. He's been a great comfort to me. I couldn't have lasted here without his assistance.'

Nadia nodded. 'I have friends like him, Berbers, Arabs and men of French descent. It's impossible to exist without them. There are times when their help is invaluable.'

'Ali is going to get you out by boat to Lisbon. You will be safe in Portugal and it won't be difficult for you to get to Switzerland.'

Nadia was frowning. 'What about you? I assumed you were coming with me.'

'I did intend to, but you can see how

things are here. I can't leave Eve and Tommy. I have to see they are safe.'

'It will be dangerous for you after I have gone. They will know you engineered my escape and will think I'm taking the information out of the country. You won't stand a chance!'

'Don't think I haven't thought about it.' Dean smiled grimly. 'For the love of Mike, Nadia! I'm only human. What do you want me to do?'

'I can't decide for you. You will do what is right. I'm not going to influence you. But that doesn't mean I'm not anxious about you.'

'I know. Sorry, my dear. I'm a bit on edge.'

'You don't have to apologise. I know the feeling only too well. I'm surprised at you, though. You have seemed so confident until now.'

'My own safety doesn't worry me. I'm suddenly aware that I'm responsible for three other lives. It's terrifying now I come to think of it.'

Nadia grinned. 'You will get over it.

Tommy and Eve aren't in any danger.'

'Not at the moment.' Dean stared at her, then said quietly, 'Supposing I did come with you to Lisbon? Imagine what it would be like for Eve. Samira for one would be suspicious. Eve would have to get out mighty quickly to avoid being interrogated.'

Nadia nodded her head. 'She and Tommy would be held as hostages.'

'That's what made me change my mind about coming with you. The three months aren't up yet. We needn't change our original plan too much. You stay put in Switzerland and if we are lucky the rest of us will join you there later.'

'In three weeks' time? Okay, I'm used to fending for myself. You are sure you can trust Ali-ben-Ahmed?'

'Definitely. He's extremely grateful to you. You have saved many of his Moslem friends from being massacred.'

'We don't know that for sure.'

'We would have heard if anything had started and we wouldn't have been left alone. I bet they were expecting you to contact me. Now they are waiting for me to make a move.'

'Yes. It's obvious they suspect I have found out about them. The three attempts on my life prove that.'

'It looks that way. Yet there may be another reason.'

Nadia smiled wryly. 'You think I have that many enemies?'

Dean shook his head. 'You've passed on other information. That would be sufficient reason. What beats me is why nothing has happened here.'

'It's not so easy. The police are alerted if anyone is killed or injured. They would ask questions and round up the rogues they keep records on. Too many would be drawn into their net. Why stir up trouble when they have us together where they can keep an eye on us?'

'I guess you are right,' Dean said thoughtfully. 'That was why I had to stay in Tangier, wasn't it?'

'Sure, to keep them quiet and less

suspicious.' Nadia was silent for a few seconds, then asked quietly, 'How long will I have to wait?'

'Ali mentioned a week. His boat ought to be back in port by then. He thought it would be too risky to recall it.'

'What kind of vessel is it?'

'A trader. Ali's a merchant, remember?'

'It sounds simple. The difficulty will be in smuggling me aboard. With Samira in the house and others outside watching, it's going to be tricky.'

'I've thought of a way, but I haven't worked out the details yet.'

Nadia looked more relaxed. 'That leaves you with two weeks more. That's not so bad.'

'Make a few engagements for the weeks ahead,' Dean advised her.

'How can I do that? You won't allow me to go to the Country Club.'

'Eve is very friendly with Evan. He's taken her to the club. Find out about future dances, parties and so on. Buy tickets or promise to attend the functions. Do it casually. You don't want to make him curious. Mention it when Evan comes to the house so that Samira can hear. It will quieten her suspicions if she thinks you are making plans for a social life.'

Nadia smiled faintly. 'Poor Evan! It might make him feel foolish.'

Dean shrugged his shoulders. 'He's going to be upset anyway when Eve goes. If they are serious about one another they will correspond. They could arrange to meet afterwards.'

'It's obvious Evan is serious, but do you think Eve cares for him?'

'How would I know?' Dean spoke irritably. 'In a situation like this it's wiser not to conjecture. Let time be the factor. Eve may have an entirely different slant on things in a few weeks' time.'

'So may we all!' Nadia chuckled. 'For the last two months I've lived from day to day, never allowing myself to consider the future.'

'I know. With fear at your elbow it couldn't have been easy.' Dean gave her a sympathetic smile. 'Soon all that will be left behind. You have a new life looming ahead of you.'

'Do you know something?' Nadia said seriously. 'I'm going to enjoy it a whole lot more. All the tiny things most people take for granted. Being able to walk down the road without turning one's head to see who is following; being able to talk openly without fear of being overheard.'

Dean nodded. 'I know exactly what you mean. I couldn't get used to it at first. Now I sometimes wonder whether there is another existence.'

'There is, especially for you. It was a lot to ask of you. And you couldn't have been happy about risking your neck for the sake of something which didn't really concern you.' Nadia stood up, then leaned down to kiss him impulsively on the cheek. 'I shall never forget what you have done and you can count on me if you ever need any help.'

Dean laughed awkwardly. 'There's no need to get maudlin. I did what I could because there wasn't much choice. Be off with you before I disgrace myself by becoming as sentimental as you are.'

When Nadia had gone Dean did not attempt to find a book to read as he sometimes did before going to bed. He sat in his chair staring ahead, his forehead creased with deep concentration. And it was nearly an hour later before he rose stiffly to his feet, turned out the lights and left the room.

6

Nadia lost no time over following Dean's advice. The next day she insisted on treating Tommy and Eve to lunch at the restaurant where Evan preferred to eat and, to the young man's delight, she invited him to dinner that evening at Dean's house. Eve was pleased for Evan had often taken Tommy and herself out and she had regretted not being able to return his hospitality.

Uncertain about Dean's reaction at having Evan's company sprung on him, Eve looked at him intently several times during the meal that night, but could see no signs of annoyance. This surprised her greatly, for she had guessed he did not feel very friendly towards the young man. Either he did not mind Evan being there or he was hiding his feelings extremely well.

For Eve it was both an interesting and disturbing evening. Evan made no attempt to hide his pleasure at being there and spoke freely and at length about the Country Club and the forthcoming social events. Eve encouraged him; something she would not have done so naturally if she had known why Nadia had asked him to come to dinner.

'I suppose it's no good asking you to come?' Evan asked, looking at Eve after he had mentioned a cocktail party due to take place the following evening.

Nadia said quickly, 'We have made plans for most evenings this week, but if there is anything special the following week we might come. Didn't you say that there was a tennis dance on Tuesday?'

'Yes,' Evan replied eagerly. 'There aren't many tickets left. Can I reserve some for you?'

'Two will be enough.' Nadia smiled. 'Dean isn't keen. He has some important engagements that week. Eve and I can come. Get the tickets and I will pay for them next time I see you.'

'There's no need to do that!' Evan exclaimed.

'I insist. We won't come otherwise.'

Evan grinned. 'Very well. There's a supper dance on the Friday. That will be my treat.'

'You can take Eve. I will pay for myself.'

Evan smiled at Eve, who was having difficulty in hiding her astonishment. 'I shall be looking forward to next week. I have been longing to escort you to some of the parties.'

Samira had been in the room during most of the conversation and Dean had been watching her curiously. Then, when he noticed that she was about to leave with a tray of dishes, he said quickly, 'It's time you thought about going to the club, Nadia. As we intend to settle here we ought to attend the social functions. It's a pity that I have been too busy to keep up. As you know, I used to go to the club frequently. It will be real nice taking you there and introducing you to all my friends. My business affairs ought to ease up soon and I shall have more time to spare for you. It's lucky you have Eve to keep you company. But she will be going back to England at the end of the month.'

The door closed behind Samira. Dean's eyes twinkled, for he had been aware that she had lingered in the room long enough to listen to what he had to say. She would pass it on to her employers and give them an entirely wrong impression of how things really were. Unfortunately he was so engrossed with the success of his plan that he failed to realise how upset Eve was looking.

His last remark had been like a sword thrust to her heart and she was fighting to keep back the stinging tears. Of course she knew that she would have to leave eventually. But Dean had made it sound so final and he had spoken so uncaringly. I'm a fool for allowing myself to be hurt because of a casual remark, she told herself sadly. He's going to marry Nadia. Naturally he doesn't care how I feel!

Evan, who had spoken to her once, repeated the question when he saw her glance at him, 'You don't have to go, do you, Eve! You could stay in an hotel for a few weeks. There's another religious holiday coming up soon and I shall be free. We could take trips out of the city; even have a few days away.'

She laughed lightly. 'It sounds very tempting. I would enjoy a few more weeks in Tangier. And I would be free to do as I pleased.'

Dean said curtly, 'Don't make any plans yet. There will be plenty of time after the wedding.' He saw her wince and cursed himself for being so brutal. Naturally she was surprised and shocked at the changes which were taking place. But any softening up on his part might endanger all their lives. He could not turn back. There was too much at stake to weaken now. It was terribly important that Eve should know nothing of what was afoot.

When Samira returned with the dessert, Nadia was talking to Evan, telling him what she intended to do after she was married. The Arab woman took an unconscionable time arranging the glass dishes on the table and even went so far as to set out forks and spoons which would not be needed. Dean watched her with interest, a faint amused smile hovering over his lips.

'I've had a post offered me at the hospital,' Nadia was saying, ignoring Samira. 'I wouldn't care to give up my work entirely.'

'You are lucky,' Evan commented. 'So many of the wives are bored. I think it is an excellent idea.'

Eve listened in silence. She had eaten very little, unable to swallow the food because of a burning sensation in her throat. She had an overwhelming desire to announce that she would be leaving Tangier before the wedding, but could not bring herself to interrupt the conversation. They would all look at her in astonishment and in her agitation she wouldn't be able to give a logical reason for leaving. Nadia might guess why she wanted to go and would feel sorry for her. And pity would be the last straw! I have to keep my unhappiness to myself, she thought. But for how long, I wonder? The agony of sitting here listening patiently is almost unbearable!

To Eve the meal seemed unending. Even Samira was dragging it out with her uncalled for incompetence; forgetting to set out enough dessert dishes, taking glasses off the table when they were needed and having to be reminded that they needed more Vichy water. What's got into her? Eve asked herself in bewilderment, puzzled because none of the others appeared to mind. I'm the only one who's not enjoying this meal. If only it would finish!

When Evan suggested a stroll after they had drunk Samira's too-sweetened coffee, Eve eagerly grasped at the chance to escape from the house for a while.

Dean frowned and said bluntly,

'There's no need for that. Aren't you tired, Eve?'

'No. I feel like some fresh air,' she said defensively.

Nadia nudged Dean with her elbow and he answered with a little more warmth. 'Okay, but don't keep her out too long, Evan.'

Eve ran up to her room to fetch her coat, for the evenings were cool after the sun went down. She joined Evan outside the front door. They walked up the path and along the tree-lined avenue without speaking and had nearly reached the end of the road before Evan exclaimed angrily:

'I don't know how you put up with that man! Every time he speaks to you it's an order. He's not your keeper! Surely you can go for a walk without obtaining his permission!'

'He didn't mean it that way,' Eve said quietly. 'He's been very lenient. On the whole I do what I like.'

'It doesn't sound like it. He doesn't own you. He's engaged to Nadia. He's a queer chap. You know before Nadia came here I thought he was interested in you. I could understand him not wanting me to take you out then, but now the picture's different. He's got no right to interfere in your private life!'

'He doesn't.' Eve laughed lightly. 'I expect he feels responsible for me. He's my employer and I'm in a foreign country. I think that most men would feel the way he does. It doesn't mean anything. If I was at home he probably wouldn't worry who my friends were or where I went.'

'He was more friendly towards me this evening,' Evan remarked thoughtfully. 'Sometimes I've had the impression that he dislikes me intensely.'

'You're too sensitive. Dean is a very busy man. He is abrupt at times, but I'm sure he's not aware of it.'

'You are too kind-hearted,' Evan said gruffly. 'Do you know this is the first time we have been alone together?' He put his arm around her waist and drew her towards him. Eve stayed there for a few minutes then edged away.

'We ought to go back, Evan,' she said quietly. 'Tommy might wake up.'

'Nadia will see to him. We've only been out ten minutes!'

'It will be another ten before we get back.' Eve smiled. 'You forget that I've been walking for most of the afternoon. My feet are beginning to ache.'

'Very well. You are making excuses, I know, but I will forgive you this time. You can make it up to me next week. Perhaps we shall be able to snatch a few hours for ourselves. I've so much I want to discuss with you.'

'You have been a good friend, Evan,' Eve said diplomatically. 'I'm very grateful to you.'

'I want us to be more than friends. I've never felt this way about a girl before. It's so frustrating, sensing this mysterious unwillingness on your part to meet me halfway.'

'I haven't found it easy to forget that I'm here to look after Tommy. It's a great responsibility.'

'Too great,' Evan said gloomily. 'Here we are back again and we haven't said anything about the future. I'm certainly learning the art of patience if nothing else!'

Eve ignored his complaints and opened the door quickly. 'I'm going up to my room. Would you tell Nadia and Dean?'

And before he could protest she ran up the flight of stairs. She gained the landing gasping for breath but conscious of enormous relief that the evening was over.

Two days later at breakfast Dean mentioned that an Arab friend had invited all of them to share a '*diffa*' at his home that evening. And when Tommy asked what that was, explained that it was a Moroccan meal.

'Does he live in a tent? Is his home in the desert?' the boy asked excitedly.

Dean chuckled. 'No, sorry to disappoint you. I told you before that Ali-ben-Ahmed has an attractive house on the outskirts of Tangier. It's a strange mixture of the old Moroccan idea of comfort plus the modern gadgets. From the outside it's a shiny white cube set in a well-ordered garden. In the centre there's a large patio with brilliant tropical flowers set against the white-washed walls of the house. Unfortunately as it will be dark you won't see any of that.'

'Shall we be allowed to eat with the men?' Eve asked curiously.

Dean's eyes twinkled. 'Ali has more advanced ideas than the older generation. His wife does not cover her face and she often wears European dress. Even so, you will find their customs a little different from ours. But you won't be shut away with the women of the house-hold. That I can guarantee. Ali prefers to have his womenfolk around him and enjoys the company of pretty girls.'

'That's a comfort.' Nadia winked at Eve. 'I've been to so many '*diffas*' and it's real boring after the novelty has worn off. There are so many women in the average home; mother, mother-in-law, sisters, grandmothers and innumerable aunts as well as the daughters of the house-hold. I can never understand how they all manage to live together in harmony.'

'Perhaps they don't,' Eve remarked with a light laugh.

'I don't think there is much friction,' Dean said seriously. 'They have been brought up that way. The older generation had little freedom and became resigned to living with their relations. They were taught to obey from childhood. Not a bad thing, I guess.'

'Be careful!' Nadia laughed. 'That's a typical male remark. Secretly you would like us to be slaves.'

'I didn't say so.' Dean grinned. 'I'm not going to be trapped into an argument about women's rights. It's too lengthy a subject.'

'Cautious, isn't he?' Nadia smiled at Eve. 'What shall we do today?'

'We've seen the museums and most

of the town,' Eve said thoughtfully. 'I think Tommy would enjoy a few hours on the beach. We can have lunch out, then go to the Country Club for a game of tennis.'

Nadia frowned slightly. 'I will come to the beach with you, but I don't fancy the club. We could drive out to Rabat. It's a dull road but fast.'

Dean shook his head. 'No, Nadia. Stay in Tangier.'

'It will have to be the Medina then,' Eve said.

'I would rather you didn't go to the Medina for a few days. Come back here after lunch. As we intend going out this evening it might be as well to have a quiet spell on the patio.'

As Nadia did not protest Eve said nothing more. But she did think that Dean was being very restrictive. Come to think of it, he always seemed happier if they were together in the house. Not for the first time she wondered why Dean had become such a recluse. He had said that it was his business that prevented him from going out, but Eve did not entirely believe this. Evan had mentioned that Dean had been a keen golf player, yet to Eve's knowledge he had not played all the time she had been in Tangier. Neither had he attended the Country Club or left Tangier.

The day passed pleasantly enough. Nadia had warned Tommy not to tell Samira that they were going out that evening. It was the woman's night off and that was why Dean had arranged for them to go then. Samira would be off the premises before they left. No doubt there would be someone watching outside the house, but he planned to leave by the back entrance. Ali had offered to have a car waiting for them in the next avenue. If he left his car parked outside the house it might give the impression that they were all at home.

At six o'clock Eve took Tommy to the bathroom so that she could wash him and change his clothes. This did not take long, for he was as eager as she was to be ready in time. So far Eve had only seen Morocco as a tourist, but now she would have a chance to meet an Arab family at home. She gave Tommy a book to look at in their bedroom whilst she took a shower and slipped on a white dress she had not worn before. It looked well with her cloud of dark hair and made her eyes look very green. As she went down the stairs with Tommy she was conscious of looking her best and was rewarded when she caught a flash of admiration in Dean's blue eyes.

Eve had quite a jolt when she saw what Nadia was wearing; a dark blue trouser suit with a thin red sweater. She looked smart, but not exactly suitable for a dinner date.

Eve glanced at Dean. 'Ought I to have worn something less dressy?' she asked doubtfully.

He smiled and shook his head. 'Your outfit is fine. Take no notice of Nadia. She's a law unto herself.'

Curiously Eve watched him go round

the house, switching on the lights, wondering if he was acting absent-mindedly, for the sun had not disappeared entirely and only a few shadows had crept across the patio.

'Would you leave a light on in your bedroom, Eve?' Dean asked. 'I want it to look as if we are at home this evening.'

'You don't want anyone to know where we are going?' She hesitated, then asked in a puzzled fashion, 'How are you going to leave without being seen?'

'Out the back way.' He glanced at his wrist-watch. 'We have another fifteen minutes. I will see if there is anyone snooping about out there. I've never seen anyone, but I would rather make sure.'

When Eve returned from her room Nadia was coming from the den. She had her large handbag slung over her shoulder and was carrying a small case.

'My medical equipment,' she explained when she noticed Eve staring at her.

'Are you expecting someone to be ill?'

'No, but I prefer to take it with me,' Nadia drawled casually. 'The house might be burgled and some of the instruments I couldn't replace over here.'

Dean came back then and Eve had to suppress her questions. Nadia often puzzled her and tonight was no exception. Although she could detect nothing unusual in her manner, Eve could sense that something was not right.

The vehicle which was to pick them up was waiting for them in the next avenue, and they were slightly out of breath by the time they reached it. A man in a loose-sleeved, white *jellaba* with a red *fez* on his head was leaning against a large modern car. He straightened when he saw them hurrying towards him and quickly opened the rear door.

'Ali!' Dean exclaimed. 'I didn't expect you to come.'

Eve studied the man curiously, noting that he was wearing a light grey lounge suit beneath the *jellaba*. Many men wore these loose top garments for they protected their suits from sand storms and rain. Many of them were waterproof and could be bought in various colours. Ali was a tall, impressive man, light skinned and lean of face. His haughty expression and suave manner caused Eve to be a little in awe of him at first.

The Arab was urging them to hurry and appeared relieved when they were all inside the car. 'It was no trouble to collect you,' he said gravely. 'I have friends who live close by, so it would seem natural for me to visit this sector. That is why I suggested this avenue.'

Eve pulled her fluffy green coat across her shoulders and fastened it, using it as a cape. It was becoming cooler and the leather seats felt cold against her shoulders. As they drove through the city she was amazed to see so many people strolling along the pavements. Many of the houses were shuttered, but the night club quarter was ablaze with lights. Couples were hurrying into restaurants and clubs, welcomed by a blare of music. When they had left the city behind them the perfume from the flowering trees and shrubs in the walled gardens of Moroccan mansions drifted into the car.

Dean had told Eve that it was a great honour to be invited to a Moslem household, for although he was friendly outside his home, the head of the household guarded his privacy with traditional persistency. But she soon found that a guest was accepted with a warmth and friendliness which was almost embarrassing. It was as if the hosts were saying, 'This is your home. We are the guests.'

When they entered the large, white stone house built around a square patio, Ali divested himself of his *jellaba, fez* and shoes and stepped into a pair of red *babouches*. He paused at the entrance to a room where guests were entertained and beckoned them to come in.

Nadia went first, but did not step on to the sumptuous, brightly coloured rug which covered most of the floor until she had removed her shoes. Taking a cue from her, Eve knelt to remove Tommy's sandals and then slipped out of her own shoes. Dean was doing the same. Then, shoeless, they walked across the rug and took their places on a cushioned bench close to one of the walls.

A few minutes later a young, fine-looking woman wearing an elegant *kaftan* entered and gracefully walked across to them.

Ali introduced her. 'My wife, Fauzia,' he said gravely.

Dean, who had met her before, smilingly presented Nadia, Eve and Tommy to her.

'We are happy that you could come,' Fauzia said with a warm smile. 'Ali has spoken of you. I hope you are enjoying Tangier.' She made a sign to the maid who had followed her into the room.

The brown-faced girl gave them

serviettes, then set in front of them a table which looked like a tray on legs. Then she disappeared and returned with water in a copper jug and a cake of soap. Tommy was intrigued with this ceremony of washing hands and Eve was delighted that he behaved so well and did not fidget as she dried his hands on the towel which the maid held out to him.

'We will not frighten you too much,' Ali remarked with a faint smile as he poured white wine into crystal goblets. 'I asked Fauzia to prepare a simple meal.'

Eve noticed that he did not have a glass for himself or his wife and remembered being told that most Moroccans do not drink with their meals. Then when the *tajin* appeared and she realised that they were expected to eat it with their fingers she became nervous in case Tommy dis-graced himself. Luckily he did not seem too keen on the meat, which had been cooked in sauce, and ate very little of it.

The *kebabs* which followed were easier to handle. Eve had eaten them before in the Medina at an open air café. Different kinds of meat impaled on skewers were less difficult to contend with, although the blue smoke coming from the grilling meat was a little overpowering.

'These should be eaten outdoors,' Fauzia hastened to explain. 'But they are a traditional dish and most people enjoy them.'

'Why do they taste so delicious?' Eve asked. 'If we cooked meat over charcoal we wouldn't get this flavour.'

Fauzia chuckled. 'We pickle the meat for hours in tomato juice, spices, onions and herbs.'

Ali placed a skewer of *kebabs* on a *kesrah*, a soft bread roll, poured gravy over it, and pressed down the top of the roll. Then he handed it to Tommy, who had been gazing at him with a fascinated expression.

'There you are, little one! That should fill you up.' He glanced at Eve, who was holding Tommy's serviette for him. 'We often have French dishes, but as you are a stranger to our country we thought a Moroccan *diffa* might interest you.'

'That was kind of you,' Eve said smilingly. 'Our housekeeper does cook Moroccan dishes sometimes, but Mr Rimmer isn't keen on them.'

'They don't taste like these,' Nadia hastened to say. 'The meat she buys is so tough and her desserts are so sweet.'

'She uses camel meat, no doubt,' Ali remarked. He saw Eve shudder and smiled. 'To you I suppose it's on the same level as horsemeat. My wife and I are not partial to it, but the poor welcome it.'

Fresh fruit followed, much to Eve's relief. She had been afraid that sweet pastries would have been served and those, she knew, none of them would fancy. They washed their fingers again and the table was removed.

Fauzia stood up and said politely, 'Ali and Mr Rimmer wish to talk so I will take the ladies and Tommy to drink tea with my family. Would you follow me, please?'

Eve glanced at Nadia, saw her nod her head, and guessed that they were expected to leave the men to themselves.

'This is the time I hate,' Nadia whispered, making sure that her hostess was too far away to hear.

The room they were ushered into appeared to be full of women of all ages. Introductions were made, but Eve took in very few of the names. Seated on cushions on the floor, they were given sweet mint tea to drink and were bombarded with questions. Two children, older than Tommy, took him aside and showed him their books. Both boys were dressed in European clothes, but the women wore *kaftans*.

'They have modern undies beneath them,' Nadia explained to Eve, who had made some comment about them. 'I expect they wear dresses and coats when they go out. The *kaftan* is a useful garment, for it buttons down the front and is long.'

'We use housecoats, so there's not much difference,' Eve said.

'I think the *kaftan* is more elegant. I have two myself. Be sure to buy one before you leave Tangier.'

'Yes. I've been meaning to. But I get scared when I try to buy anything. The prices are always so high to start with.'

'You are expected to haggle. Cut the price in half and you will be about right. Some of the European stores have set prices but their goods may not always be the ones you prefer.'

One of the women asked Nadia about her work and she soon had the attention of the rest of them. This gave Eve the opportunity to scan the paintings which decorated the white walls. They were modern and very colourful and some she guessed had been painted by the young people. Pots of flowering plants were arranged along the borders of the room. Eve recognised a camellia tree and was surprised to see a few geraniums. These gave her a pang of nostalgia and for a few minutes she was back in the street in London where she had lived with her sister.

Then Fatima, a teenage girl, light-skinned with curly black hair and soft brown eyes, spoke to her, and Eve found herself discussing the differences of education in their countries. Eve discovered that the girls of the household attended a French Lycée, and although they were Moslems, received instruction in the Christian religion.

'My parents wish me to have a broader outlook than they had,' Fatima explained, noticing that Eve was surprised. The girl spoke English well, but with a French accent. 'So many girls marry at seventeen. My mother does not wish me to do that.'

'Do you intend to take up a profession?' Eve asked.

The girl nodded. 'It will be difficult, you understand. There is a great prejudice against women who compete in the business and professional world. I am lucky because my father can offer me a position in his firm. But first I have to pass exams.'

'Do you wear a uniform at school?'

'Yes.' Fatima's dark eyes sparkled. 'We also wear mini-skirts and stretch pants if we wish. My aunts do not approve, but they can do nothing because my parents are agreeable. The older women do not understand what is happening in the world outside.'

'Did you paint some of those pictures?'

'No, my sister did. She hopes to go to Paris in a few months to attend a college where she can learn to improve her painting.'

Nadia, who had moved away from Eve, came across to her and helped her to rise from the cushion she had been sitting on. 'We have to go. Fauzia says that Dean is waiting for us.'

Eve smiled a farewell at the women and, with Tommy held securely by the hand, followed Nadia out of the room.

Ali-ben-Ahmed greeted them gravely. Dean was looking uneasy and Eve wondered why he cast so many anxious glances at Nadia, who was looking remarkably relaxed.

Dean said quietly, 'Take Tommy out to the car, Eve.'

Ali led the way from the room and Eve began to move after him. She was expecting Nadia to follow and turned at the door to see where she was. A pang of dismay smote her as she watched Dean lean over and kiss Nadia hard on the mouth, and it was a few seconds before she was able to pull herself together. Dazed and shaken, she hurried after Tommy and Ali, and was sitting in the back of the car when Dean left the house and climbed in the front seat next to Ali.

'Isn't Nadia coming with us?' Eve asked after Dean had slammed the door shut.

He looked back at her and shook his head, then, after a swift glance at Tommy, who was half asleep, put his finger to his lips.

So that was the meaning for the embrace, Eve mused in some bewilderment. He was saying goodbye to her. Perhaps she's going to stay with Fauzia for a few days. But why didn't she tell me?

'Samira hasn't returned yet,' Dean remarked after he had been up to the housekeeper's room and glanced into the other rooms. 'That's a slice of luck! She won't know we've been out.'

Eve was eyeing him curiously, longing to ask why Nadia had not come back with them, but Tommy was propping himself up against her in an effort to keep awake.

'I will carry him up for you,' Dean said and, picking the boy up, carefully led the way up the stairs.

'Thanks, Dean. I can manage now,' Eve assured him after he had put Tommy on to his bed. 'I won't bath him tonight. He's asleep already. It would be a shame to wake him.'

'You look as if you could do with a sleep yourself!' Dean paused at the door. 'I will explain about Nadia in the morning. Don't let on to Samira that she's not here.'

Eve nodded. There was nothing she could find to say. He was still looking so very anxious and it was affecting her also.

Evidently he was aware of her distress, for he said gently before he went out and closed the door, 'Don't worry. Everything will seem different in the morning.'

7

Eve awoke the next morning with the uneasy sensation that something was wrong. Then she remembered that Nadia had not come back to the house and for the first time since she had come to live with Tommy and Dean she felt afraid. It was silly, she knew, for no one had threatened or injured her. Yet, try as she might, she could not shake off the awful feeling she had that something had happened or was about to happen. Perhaps it was because she guessed that Dean and Nadia were in danger that she had this sense of foreboding. Was that why Dean had left Nadia at the Arab's house? Did he think she would be safer there?

What are they mixed up in? Eve asked herself nervously. Dean had said it was nothing criminal. It couldn't be anything to do with Nadia's patients, could it? No, of course not. That wouldn't link Dean and Nadia together. Whatever they were involved in, it was something serious. If it hadn't been, Dean would have given Samira the sack when he found out she was spying on the household. At first I imagined it was something to do with Dean's business affairs, Eve thought. And I never really considered it to be of much consequence. Now I know I was wrong. It is serious and Samira is dangerous. That's why Dean would never go very far away. His life has been threatened, too. That must be it. Oh, dear, I am worried now, terrified in fact!

Trying to solve the mystery at such an early hour in the morning was ridiculous, Eve decided. She had given herself a headache and frightened herself as well. It's all supposition anyway, she told herself practically. I expect I've got it all wrong. It may be something quite simple.

As Tommy was sleeping soundly she took the opportunity to take a shower before she dressed. She could hear someone moving about downstairs and guessed that Samira was preparing the breakfasts.

Dean was waiting for Eve and Tommy in the living-room. He was wearing a light-brown suit with a cream shirt and dark tie. Eve presumed that he was going to his office and was relieved to see that he looked less taut than the evening before.

When she came in with Tommy he shut the door and said in a low voice, 'Come out to the patio.'

She nodded, left the boy playing on the floor with his toy camel, and stepped out on to the paving stones beyond the french windows. Sunlight was beginning to thrust warm fingers across one side of the walled garden a few feet away from the patio and Eve wandered over there so that she could benefit from the heat of the sun. Dean glanced at her once or twice as he went with her.

'I guess you are puzzled because I did

not tell you Nadia was going.'

Eve looked startled. 'Has she gone for good?'

'Yes. Ali is going to get her out of the country.'

'I knew you were worried about her.'

'She was in danger all the time she was here.'

'She didn't reveal her fear.'

Dean smiled. 'Nadia has grown accustomed to it. She never allowed herself to think too much about it. I've never known anyone quite like her. No, that's not strictly true. I do know of one other person. They are two of a kind.'

'She has left most of her things behind!' Eve exclaimed.

'That was intentional. Samira has to believe that Nadia is here.' He hesitated, then continued awkwardly, 'I shall need your help, Eve.'

'It's going to be difficult to convince Samira. She's so curious.'

'I know. But it will only be for a few days, I hope. By then Nadia ought to be safe.'

Eve thought for a moment, then said doubtfully, 'I could pretend that Nadia is ill. I could tell Samira and take some orange juice to the den. I could say she doesn't fancy anything else.'

'That's an excellent idea! Have you any suggestions for later on. Samira will want to go in the den to tidy it so that she can satisfy her curiosity.'

'I could lock it. There is a key, isn't there? I noticed Tommy playing with it and took it away from him.'

'It will look suspicious if we lock the door.'

'Not if I say it's to prevent Tommy from disturbing Nadia.'

'It means you won't be able to go out much. Luckily the den doesn't open out on to the patio. There's only one door.'

'If I continue to take meals into the den that would seem authentic.'

Dean grinned. 'What are you going to do with them?'

'Eat them myself.' She laughed. 'You will have to have some of my dinner at night. I can pretend that Nadia has caught some bug or other and is unable to eat much.'

'That ought to keep Samira quiet for a few days.'

Eve frowned. 'This is going to alter your plans, isn't it?' She broke off in some confusion. 'I mean, you intended to get married soon.'

Dean nodded, glanced at her swiftly and looked away. 'All that talk about our future in Tangier was window dressing. I'm sorry we had to deceive Evan. If our plans succeed you won't be able to keep your dates with him, Eve.'

In a puzzled voice she asked, 'Wouldn't it look more natural if I went to the Country Club with him?'

'You can go this week if you wish, but I have plans for you and Tommy. You may not have to stay much longer.' He glanced at her apologetically. 'I'm real sorry, Eve. I feel I'm making a mess of your life.'

'It doesn't matter,' she said quickly. 'You are telling me I have to leave?'

'Not on your own. I want you to take

Tommy to Switzerland. You remember the address?'

'Yes.' She looked subdued. 'What about you? Are you going to stay behind?'

'I have to, but don't worry. My time is nearly up now.'

All the colour left her face and she was stricken with fear.

Dean took her hand. 'For the love of Mike, Eve! What is it? What's the matter with you?'

'It was the way you spoke. You made me afraid.'

He laughed. 'Buck up! Nothing is going to happen to any of us. I've promised Nadia I shall see her before the month is out. But first I have to get you and Tommy away from here.'

'I suppose I can't tell Evan I'm going?'

He shot a swift enquiring look at her. 'No,' he said gruffly. 'Not yet. Perhaps the day before you leave. I don't want to make things too unpleasant for you. Now, shall we go in? We don't want

Samira to go looking for Nadia, do we?'

Actually, deceiving Samira was easier than Eve had anticipated. When told the doctor was ill, an expression of horror flashed across the Arab woman's face.

'Is it infectious?' she asked. 'There is much sickness to be caught in the Medina. Recently two women died after eating food they bought from a stall.'

Eve nodded. 'I think it might be. She has a rash and she complains of stomach pains. We did eat out yesterday.' She noticed that the woman's hands were shaking as she placed the teapot on the kitchen table and hastened to add, 'There's no need for you to go near her, Samira. Fevers are usually contagious. I've been inoculated for most illnesses. I will look after her. I know what to do.'

'It is not only from coming in contact with the stricken one. There will be her clothes to wash and her dishes. I have much knowledge of such things. I have

191

lived through two epidemics.' She shuddered. 'I would not care to see another.'

'There is no need for you to touch anything belonging to Doctor Green,' Eve assured her. 'I will do her laundry and wash her dishes.'

Samira nodded. 'That is good. If you had not said that, I not stay.'

After that positive declaration Eve wondered whether she had acted too hastily. If she had not offered to nurse Nadia, Samira might have left. And that would have made things much easier. She remained doubtful until she had spoken to Dean that evening. Whilst they were drinking their coffee she explained what had happened that morning.

'I was utterly amazed,' Eve said. 'The woman was petrified. Apparently she's terrified of anything infectious.'

'That figures. It's so easy to catch something in the markets. And it's not always easy to detect the germ in time to save the victim.' He smiled with satisfaction. 'It makes our task easier.'

'If I hadn't suggested that I look after Nadia, Samira would have left. I feel annoyed with myself.'

'Don't blame yourself,' Dean said firmly. 'She wouldn't have gone until she had someone to take her place.'

Eve sighed with relief. 'I felt awfully mean deceiving her like that. I get on fairly well with her. I think she trusts me.'

'Don't bet on it! That woman trusts no one. She's paid to keep her eyes and ears open. Never forget that, Eve.'

'I won't,' Eve replied seriously. 'I would never forgive myself if I endangered your life.'

Dean leaned across and put his hand on her arm; an appreciative, affectionate gesture which warmed Eve's heart. She smiled back at him, forgetting for the moment that he had asked Nadia to marry him.

Evan called at the house the next day. Eve thought he seemed put out when she opened the door to him, but she did not remark on it and asked him to come in.

'Why didn't you turn up at the restaurant as we arranged?' he asked in hurt tones. 'When you didn't come yesterday I was certain you would turn up today. I waited for as long as I dared, then I had to get back to my class.'

Eve looked dismayed. 'I'm sorry, Evan. I forgot I had made a date with you. Nadia was taken ill yesterday and I haven't been out except to take Tommy for a short walk.'

'Oh, I'm sorry. Is it anything serious?'

'No, just a tummy upset. But it has scared Samira. She won't go near her. That's why I have to stay in.'

Evan threw himself into an armchair. His face was gloomy and Eve could sense that he was preparing to be unpleasant.

'Nadia is Dean's fiancée. Why doesn't he look after her?'

'He has to go to his office every day. I don't have much to do. I couldn't leave

Nadia by herself.'

'I think it's a darn shame! You will be leaving soon and I wanted to see you every minute I could.'

Eve chuckled. 'Don't look so cross, Evan. You are seeing me now.'

'What's the good of five minutes or so? I had planned to take you and Tommy out for the day tomorrow.'

'I can't go, but you could take Tommy. It would help me.'

'Thanks for nothing,' he said bitterly. 'You don't seem a bit concerned. You don't care whether you see me or not.'

'That's not fair. I've told you I enjoy your company.'

'Then tell Dean tonight that you intend to go out tomorrow. I'm sure he will offer to stay and look after Nadia.'

'No.' Eve stared at him in slight annoyance. 'I have offered to stay in. I can't keep changing my mind.'

'If that's how you feel there's no point in continuing our friendship.' Evan was working himself into a fury.

'You think more of Dean than you do of me!'

Eve's face whitened. 'There's no need to shout. I agree with you. You can cancel the arrangements for next week. Nadia won't be well enough to go out and I won't go without her.'

'That's it then.' Evan stood up and glared at her. 'I bet you are relieved to have such a good excuse.' He stalked to the door, then turned back, his face red and angry. 'I won't force my attentions on you. It's been a losing battle from the start. I was a fool to hope. You won't have another chance, Eve. This is goodbye!'

'Don't go like that, Evan,' Eve pleaded, her anger turning to regret because she felt guilty at deceiving him. 'I hate parting in anger.'

'If you change your mind about next week let me know,' he said heatedly. 'You can make the next move. Perhaps when you consider what you are doing you will see how unfair you have been to me. Dean employed you to look after

Tommy. You don't have to be a nurse as well!'

He twisted round, charged through the door and ran right into Dean, who was about to enter the room. Evan made no attempt to apologise, but brushed roughly by Dean and strode to the door, banging it loudly behind him.

'Sorry, Eve.' Dean looked at her uncertainly as he walked across to her. 'Did I interrupt something? Evan seemed unlike himself.'

Eve laughed shakily and sat down quickly on a chair. 'I never realised he had such a temper,' she said. 'I was supposed to meet him for lunch yesterday and I forgot.'

'Is that all?' Dean looked annoyed. 'If I had known I would have given him a piece of my mind.'

'It wasn't entirely that,' Eve said awkwardly. 'He wanted to take Tommy and me out for the day tomorrow and when I refused he took it badly.'

Dean frowned. 'You could have gone, Eve.'

'I didn't want to go. If I wasn't here Samira would think it strange and I couldn't go out and leave the den unlocked. And if I left it locked it would look peculiar.'

'I could have stayed in tomorrow. I'm clearing things up at the office. I could have gone there in the evening.'

'There's no need to alter our arrangement. Evan's temper will cool. I expect he will come back.'

Dean frowned uneasily. 'He's an obstinate man. Are you sure you don't want to go? I could get in touch with him and tell him it was a mistake.'

Eve shook her head. 'There's no point. You said that I would be leaving soon. I've cancelled the arrangements we made with Evan for next week. Now I needn't tell him I'm going.'

Dean glanced at her curiously. 'I thought you might be upset. You are taking it real well. To be honest, I'm relieved. The fewer who know about our plans the safer we shall be. You can return here when this is all over, Eve. I would willingly pay your expenses. Then you could explain to Evan why you had to be so mysterious and why you left without telling him.'

'Thank you! I think that's very generous of you. If I do decide to come back I will let you know.' Eve gave him a warm smile. She had no intention of returning to see Evan, but Dean need not know that. It would be less embarrassing for her, for she did not want Dean to guess how she felt about him. And now that Nadia had gone she constantly had to remind herself that Dean was not free.

To change the subject she said lightly, 'I thought I would wash a few of Nadia's clothes tomorrow. If she were really ill that would be the natural thing to do. Luckily she left most of her things.'

Dean nodded. 'We won't be able to keep it up much longer. I've made arrangements for you and Tommy to leave on Friday morning.'

'So soon!' Eve was unable to hide her

dismay and surprise.

'It will give us two days. I've reserved seats on the plane to Paris. When you have gone I shall say you are taking Tommy back to his aunt and you decided to have a few days in Paris en route.'

'That's going to make nonsense of all you have said to Samira!'

He sighed. 'I know. We had to alter our plans. With Nadia gone there's no sense in pretending we are going to stay on here.'

'So you did intend to settle here?' Eve frowned. 'Sorry, that was a silly question. You wouldn't have asked Anita to send Tommy out here if that was not the case.'

'It was Nadia who wanted the boy here so soon. It might have been easier if she had waited until after the wedding.'

'She was afraid that Tommy might not take to her,' Eve said quietly. 'I can understand her anxiety. Now Tommy has met her it will seem more natural for him to accept her as his new mother.'

'Sure. That would have been okay but for the change in our arrangement. Now I can see it would have been far better to have left the boy in London for a few more weeks.'

Eve said worriedly, 'What will happen to you after we have gone?'

He laughed. 'Nothing, I guess. I've survived so far. I shall find it simpler having only myself to watch out for.'

'These people who have been so interested in you . . . ' Eve paused, then continued more steadily, 'Why do they spy on you? Why don't they contact you?'

'They don't want me to leave Tangier.'

'You would put them in danger if you did go?'

'Something like that. But if I stay much longer they will discover that I've been fooling them. That's why I have to get you out. I shall follow as soon as I can.'

'Why can't you come with us?'

'If I did we would all be stopped. The men we have alienated have friends in high places. It would be easy for them to cook up some charge or other. I'm the one they want to keep here. There's no sense in involving you and Tommy.'

'I can see why you want us to go. We are another threat to your safety. I suppose they could snatch us and use us to weaken your position.'

Dean chuckled. 'I doubt whether it would come to that. You have too vivid an imagination.' Suddenly he became serious and stared at her earnestly. 'I wish your stay could have been a happier one. We could have had such a wonderful time. Three months . . . what a waste!'

Her green eyes became puzzled. 'I have enjoyed it. I shall always remember my stay in Tangier.'

He frowned. 'Sure. I had forgotten. You met Evan, didn't you.'

She turned away. His words had brought a chill to to her heart and for a

202

moment or two she fought the misery which threatened her composure.

Dean said abruptly, 'I heard Samira come in a few minutes ago. It might be a good idea to visit the den.'

Eve nodded. 'It might look better if you came also. Wait a short while. I will call out when I've made the tea. Then we can take it into the den, pretending that we are going to have it with Nadia.'

'How is Doctor Green?' Samira enquired when Eve went into the kitchen.

'She feels a little better today,' Eve replied cautiously. She noticed that the woman was about to pour hot water on to the tea bags and said quickly, 'Let it boil first!'

'You English are so fussy about your tea,' Samira grumbled. 'I can't see what difference it makes. The water is very hot.'

'You have a certain way of making your mint tea,' Eve remarked mildly.

'I make it, but you never drink it!' As Eve refrained from answering this complaint, the woman went on in a voice tinged with malice, 'Mr Rimmer does not seem very concerned about his fiancée.'

'You are wrong, Samira. He is very anxious. He keeps his anxiety well covered.' Eve smiled. 'You do the same, don't you, Samira?'

A flash of anger showed for an instant in the woman's dark eyes. 'If someone close to me was ill I would show it.'

Eve sighed. 'That was supposed to be a compliment. I'm sorry if I annoyed you.'

Samira shrugged her fat shoulders. 'It is strange, is it not, that the doctor is so quiet?'

'She sleeps most of the time. I have given her a sedative, but it will have worn off by now. Mr Rimmer and I are going to sit with her and drink our tea.'

'What about the boy?'

'He can have his in here with you.'

'He will get in my way. I have the dinner to prepare.'

'Don't bother about him then,' Eve said equably. 'He is playing out on the patio. It won't hurt him to go without. He has his supper early.'

'I have been speaking to someone who knows about medicine and he says that you ought to have a doctor to look at the patient and give us all a check up. You or Mr Rimmer may have the infection.'

'I'm sure we have not,' Eve said firmly. 'Doctor Green is improving steadily. She will be up in a day or so.'

Eve was thankful that Dean chose that moment to look in.

'It's nearly ready, Mr Rimmer,' she said cheerfully.

'I'm going in to see Nadia. Can you manage by yourself?'

'Yes. I shall only be a few minutes.'

When Eve carried the tray into the den she heard soft music being played and guessed that Dean had switched on the radio.

'Samira thinks that the patient is too quiet,' she said after Dean had closed the door.

Dean frowned. 'She's becoming suspicious. Did she say anything else?'

'Oh, yes. Someone has told her that we ought to have a doctor visit the house to make sure that we haven't caught Nadia's germs.'

'That figures.' Dean grinned. 'They would just love to send someone along to spy out the land. It's proved one thing. We couldn't keep up the pretence much longer.'

'Even so, two days will not be easy,' Eve said gravely.

'Today and tomorrow, it's not impossible.'

Eve said as she poured out the tea, 'Would you lock the door? Tommy might run in.'

Dean got up and walked to the door. 'How about Tommy?' he asked as he turned the key. 'Has he been curious about Nadia?'

'He was upset when I first mentioned Nadia's illness, but I told him she would soon be well if she stayed in bed and remained quiet. He's not mentioned it since. Children take things as they come.'

'He's very matter of fact.'

'So are most children. They don't query things like adults do. Some are more curious than others, but a child knows that if someone is ill they have to stay in bed.'

'It seems rather heartless not asking about her.'

'He has done that, but briefly. I assured him Nadia is getting better. He lost interest after that.'

Dean spooned sugar into his tea. 'I was relieved to find that he likes Nadia. It's important that they get on together.'

Eve remained silent. The topic of conversation was painful and she did not feel too sure of herself.

Dean was regarding her intently. 'Is teaching very important to you, Eve?' he asked gruffly.

She smiled. 'That's difficult to answer. My parents couldn't afford for me to stay at university to finish my exams so I had to be satisfied with teaching the lower grades. I've been a nursery teacher since I was nineteen.'

'You ought to find it a great help when you have a family of your own.'

'Perhaps. I hadn't given it much thought,' Eve said awkwardly.

Dean eyed her curiously. 'You do want to marry, Eve?'

She kept her eyes on the cup she was holding. 'Most girls do. I'm no exception.'

'I'm real pleased to hear that. I was afraid you were one of those dedicated women who prefer to care for other people's children.'

Eve smiled faintly. 'I wouldn't prefer to do that. But it might suffice if I was unable to marry.'

Dean said seriously, 'Marriage never seemed all that important until recently. Now I'm terrified that something will happen to ruin my chances.'

Eve nodded her head and gave him a swift sympathetic glance. 'I can guess how you feel. Do you think Nadia is safe?'

He straightened in his chair and there was a wary look in his blue eyes. 'I haven't heard anything to the contrary. She ought to be halfway across Europe by now.'

'Where is she making for?'

'To the hotel where you are going. Don't worry if she's not there when you arrive.'

'I'm to wait?'

'Yes. Whatever you do don't leave. You will be safe there.'

'Do you intend to join us?'

Dean smiled. 'That is my intention.'

'How long will you remain here after Tommy and I have gone?'

'No longer than I can help,' he said gravely. 'It's in the lap of the gods. I shall have to move swiftly, but whether I can get out of Morocco right away depends on what facilities there are.'

'Couldn't you fly out?'

'Someone would spot me. I'm not good at disguises and I can't play act.'

'Will Ali-ben-Ahmed help you?'

'I'm sure he will. He's been a stout friend. One day if all goes well I may be able to return the favours he's shown me.' He sighed. 'All that seems a long way off at the moment.'

'What do you plan on doing afterwards?'

His blue eyes glinted. 'Don't tempt me too much, Eve.' He chuckled. 'Who gave you a name like that? It was asking for trouble.'

She nodded. 'I used to get annoyed when I was teased.'

'By your boy friends?'

'Sometimes.' She veiled her eyes with a downward sweep of her dark lashes, wishing that he would stop gazing at her in tender amusement.

'It's a pretty name,' he said softly. 'I've never recovered from that first impression I had of you. I guess you haven't an inkling how those green eyes draw attention to you or the effect they have on a man. Yes, Eve suits you. I couldn't have chosen a better one.'

She laughed lightly, pink with embarrassment. 'Names aren't important. It's character that counts.'

He said quickly, 'You don't consider

a name important?'

'No.' She gave him a puzzled glance because he had spoken so urgently.

'I'm glad you said that,' he said gravely. 'It could have been another obstacle.'

'Could it?' she replied doubtfully, then she smiled. 'I really can't imagine why a name should cause a flutter.'

'No, you are right. It's people who matter.' He went to the window and pulled down the shade. 'We've been here long enough. The invalid ought to be allowed some rest.'

'Yes.' Eve got to her feet and picked up the tray. 'It's nearly time for Tommy's supper and I have to bath him first. He will be wondering where I am.'

As she finished speaking they heard the boy run down the hall. Eve went out quickly, leaving Dean inside.

'Here I am, Tommy,' she called out. 'Are you ready for your bath?'

'Could I have a drink? Samira won't let me in the kitchen. She's awful grumpy today.'

'Go upstairs and I will bring you a coke. You like that, don't you?'

Dean came out of the den and locked the door. 'Not too much noise, Tommy. Nadia is trying to sleep.'

'Have all her spots gone?' the boy asked curiously.

'Yes. You can see her soon.'

'Can we all go out then?'

'Maybe. Is there somewhere special you want to go?'

'I want to see the snake charmer.'

Dean chuckled and glanced at Eve. 'If you are good I will take you tomorrow.'

'Is Eve coming?'

'No,' she replied quickly. 'I shall stay with Nadia.'

'I wish she would hurry up and get well,' Tommy muttered as he turned towards the stairs. 'She promised me a ride on a camel.'

Eve was a little preoccupied as she gave Tommy his bath and prepared his supper. That conversation with Dean in the den had left her more puzzled than ever. Sometimes she could not understand him at all. It was almost as if he was trying to tell her something, then stopped at the crucial moment to have second thoughts. I suppose he's terribly worried about Nadia and it's making him careless of what he says, she thought. I get like that when I'm afraid or upset. Poor Dean . . . he must be frantic with worry. All his plans have gone wrong. Now he will have to start a new life somewhere else. I wonder whether he will be able to start up a new business easily? He's said nothing about the financial side, but I bet he's losing a lot of money. When he joins Nadia in Switzerland I shall have to return to London. I can't bear to think of it! How am I going to get through the next few months? I shall never love anyone as I do Dean. The future will be so bleak. Yet knowing that Dean is happy will be some consolation. And I have my work to go back to. It's fortunate that I enjoy teaching. Even time will help. Broken hearts mend.

Oh, dear, how foolish I'm being. It's best not to contemplate more than one day at a time. Dean and Tommy need me now. That's what is important.

Eve went down for dinner, helped Samira to wash the dishes, then told Dean that she would not stay to have coffee with him. He seemed disappointed but did not protest when she said that she ought to spend a little time in the den.

'Samira will expect me to prepare Nadia for the night,' she explained. 'She isn't going out tonight so I have to be careful.'

Dean nodded. 'Leave the light on in the den and take the key with you when you go to bed.'

'Samira always goes out after she has finished the dinner. This is the first night she has stayed in.'

'Yes. She's been told to stay with us. Be careful, Eve. Don't leave the door of the den open.'

'I won't. What time will you need Tommy tomorrow?'

'I will take him to the Medina in the morning. You can tell Samira not to bother about lunch.'

'Very well. Good night, Dean.'

'Sleep well.' He smiled and stretched out on the settee. 'I intend to keep an eye on Samira. I won't be retiring just yet.'

Eve closed the door, then went into the kitchen to prepare a glass of hot milk, giving Samira the impression that it was for Nadia.

'This ought to help her sleep,' she said as she poured out the milk. 'I shall give her a couple of tablets as well, just to keep her temperature down.'

The Arab woman eyed her curiously. 'You have done nursing before?'

'Occasionally. There's no need to worry, Samira. The fever has gone. When she feels stronger and begins to eat more she will be able to get up.'

Satisfied that she had convinced the woman, Eve went along to the den, making as much noise as she dared, pretending to make the bed and move the furniture about. Once or twice she raised her voice as if she was speaking to Nadia, then sat down to drink the hot milk herself. She remained there until she heard Samira go up to bed and when all seemed quiet she locked the den and went up to her room, taking the key with her.

8

As it was to be their last full day in Tangier, Eve and Dean decided to devote most of their time to Tommy. Dean went off with him after breakfast to the old quarter surrounding the Sultan's Palace and gardens to watch the snake charmer. It was difficult to lure a fascinated Tommy away, but when he did Dean drove farther out to the Rif coast, where they had lunch in an hotel. Afterwards they spent an exciting hour on the terrace gazing at the water-skiing.

Dean paid their bill and was crossing the grass lawn outside the hotel when a woman who had a few minutes ago alighted from a big car ran towards him.

'Dean!' she shouted in a shrill voice. 'Don't go! I want to talk to you.'

Dean cast a swift glance over his

shoulder, then grabbed Tommy and ran for his car. He had banged the doors and was driving off when the woman caught up with them. She called out again but Dean ignored her and accelerated.

'She's the lady who came to the house,' Tommy said with an amused giggle. 'I 'member her because of her hair. It's awful gold.'

Dean nodded absent-mindedly, intent on getting as far away as possible.

'Didn't you want to talk to her?' Tommy asked innocently.

'No. Eve is expecting us back. She is going to take you out this afternoon. Mrs Morgan would have delayed us.'

'She looked awful cwoss,' Tommy commented, then forgot the incident as his gaze alighted on a string of donkeys being led close to the sidewalk.

Eve was sitting on the patio when they entered the house, but got up to greet them. 'Did you enjoy yourself, Tommy?' she asked.

He nodded solemnly. 'Where are you

going to take me?'

Eve glanced at Dean and laughed. 'What energy! He doesn't look tired at all.'

Dean asked in a low voice, 'Is Samira in?'

Eve nodded. 'She didn't go out this morning.'

'That looks bad. I was hoping I could drive you down to the beach.'

'It doesn't matter. We can catch the bus at the end of the road. I'm looking forward to having a swim and being able to laze on the beach. I'm ready to go now.

'Okay. Has Samira acted at all suspiciously?'

'She tried the handle of the door to the den, but went away when she saw me watching her.'

Eve and Tommy did not have long to wait for a bus and within half an hour were taking advantage of the golden sands which sloped smoothly down to the clear blue sea. The day was warm, the sky cloudless, and Eve took every opportunity to tan herself with the sun she knew would not be so indulgent in a few days' time.

It was a relief to get away from the house for a few hours. The last two days had been a strain. Yet she was conscious of a deep sadness, for she was loath to leave Tangier, with its twisting market places, overhanging streets and tree-lined avenues set on the hills. She sat up and stared at the long, curving bay where the sea glinted with sunlight and sighed regretfully. It's a fabulous place, she thought. And it could have been perfect if only . . .

Shrugging off the poignancy of her mood, she ran down to the sparkling waters and joined Tommy, who was waving his fists at the encroaching waves which were threatening his sand castle, and soon became engrossed in helping him build another.

Not wishing to encounter Evan, who might decide to stroll down to the beach after school had finished, she left the sands at four o'clock and took

Tommy to have a drink and an ice-cream at a sidewalk café. By then Tommy was showing signs of tiredness and irritability. Firmly she refused his request that they go back to the Medina to look for storks' nests and took him to the bus stop to wait for transport back to their avenue.

When they arrived home it was too early to bath Tommy, so Eve sent him out to the patio to play. This gave her the opportunity to talk to Dean, whom she thought was looking strained and worried.

'Samira hasn't come in yet,' he told her. 'She went out soon after you did. It might be a good time to do your packing.'

Eve nodded. 'I have done some of it, but Tommy's clothes are scattered about. I'm afraid I shall have to take some of them back dirty.'

'Leave them behind. He appears to have plenty.'

'Perhaps that would be better. It will arouse Samira's suspicions if I pack everything tonight.'

Dean was not paying attention. 'I have to get back to the office. Would you mind having dinner alone tonight?'

Eve tried to hide her disappointment. She had been looking forward to having a last meal with him. 'No, of course not,' she said. 'It was good of you to stay in this afternoon.'

'It was the least I could do.' He smiled. 'I wish I could have gone with you. This has been a strange assignment for you. You've had to be so many things. I bet you never bargained for the role you've had to play.'

Her green eyes danced with amusement. 'I've never told so many white lies before. I've even surprised myself.'

'I hope it won't become a habit.' Dean grinned. 'I would have thought you would be a poor liar.'

'It's different when other people's welfare is at stake.'

'Sure. I know what you mean.' He sighed. 'Thank goodness it's nearly over. With any luck in a few days' time we can begin to behave normally.' He glanced at her intently. 'Don't look so glum! Surely you aren't sorry to leave all this?'

'To be perfectly honest, yes, I am. My life back home will seem awfully dull.'

He said swiftly, 'You don't have to go back.'

'No. I suppose I could find something to do in Switzerland,' Eve said awkwardly, aware of his strange manner and the urgency with which he had spoken. 'I needn't think of that now.'

'Are you nervous about going to Paris?' he asked, regarding her anxiously.

'Oh, no. I've been there before. I thought I would take Tommy to the Hotel Metropol. It's near the Gare du Nord. It's small but comfortable and I know my way around from there.'

'You will go by train to Montreux?'

'Yes. It will make a change and we can sleep on the train.'

'You will arrive in Montreux about seven in the morning, I guess. If you wish to stay in Paris more than one night please do so. There's no need to rush off to Switzerland.'

'I will see how Tommy feels. A stay in Paris might give him time to adjust to the travelling.'

'I think that's an excellent idea. Samira usually goes out in the mornings to shop. We can slip out then with your cases. I expect someone will note that we are making for the airfield, but we won't have to answer Samira's questions. The flight is for eleven o'clock.'

'I will be ready.'

Congratulating herself because she thought she had convinced Dean that she was not too unhappy at leaving, she went up to her room to pack most of her clothes. It did not take her long and when she had finished she called Tommy to come up for his bath. She was preparing his supper when Samira came in. The Arab woman looked surprised then pleased when Eve told her not to cook dinner that evening.

'I can have mine with Tommy,' she explained. 'Mr Rimmer has gone out and will not be back until late.'

Because Samira took her time over leaving the house the next morning, they had only enough time to drive to the airport and rush to the Paris aircraft. This left them little time for farewells. In fact Eve scarcely remembered what she or Dean had said to one another. Tommy was rather tearful and it was mainly due to him that Eve had little time to spare for her own anguish at parting with Dean.

Accommodation was available at the Metropol when she arrived there, so she booked for two nights and took the opportunity to visit some of the places she had not had time to see before. On the third day she spent a little time at the hairdresser's having a shampoo and set, and persuaded Tommy to have his head of fair hair trimmed.

It had all passed very quickly and competently, she thought that evening when, with Tommy, she boarded the couchette train en route for Switzerland. It was mainly because she could speak the French language well that all had gone so smoothly. Tommy slept soundly, but Eve, who was acutely conscious that she was coming to the end of her assignment, felt too miserable to sleep. Her heart was heavy with her longing for Dean and her mind feverishly anxious about his safety. What was happening now in Tangier? she asked herself fearfully. Would Dean be able to leave without being questioned . . . perhaps even something worse . . . tortured? These things did happen. As she was completely in the dark as to why Dean was in danger her mind became inflamed with fearful scenes and it was with great relief that she noticed that dawn was breaking.

Tommy awoke as the train slowed through the mountainous scenery. He was nearly speechless with excitement, for he had not seen mountains before.

'Do we have to go right to the top?'

he asked, with his nose glued to the window.

Eve chuckled. 'We shall go up a good way, but not too far. We might get snowed up.'

'Is that what that white stuff is?'

'Yes, snow and ice. But it's a long way up. Doesn't it look lovely with the sun shining on it?' She stood up and began to take the cases down from the rack above. 'We are nearly there, so put your jacket on.'

They took a taxi from the station and within an hour were having breakfast in the terrace restaurant of the Hotel Mignon. Eve had asked the girl who had booked them in whether a Doctor Green was staying there, but had been told that no one of that name had registered.

I had expected Nadia to have reached here before this, Eve thought with a worried frown as she helped Tommy to cherry jam. I do hope she is all right.

The hotel was in the centre of Montreux, surrounded by its own

227

beautiful gardens, and if Eve had not felt so uneasy she would have allowed Tommy to play quietly on the lawn. But she was unable to sit down for long and took the boy to the lakeside promenade. There they watched the steamers on Lac Leman and gazed at the barrier of mountains which sheltered the town. When they returned to the hotel for lunch Tommy was showing no signs of fatigue, and Eve was thankful that the boy was taking events in his stride. Eve did think it strange that he did not enquire after his daddy, but guessed that it was because he was used to living without him. Surprisingly enough, he did ask where Nadia was and whether he was going to see her again.

'Yes. We are going to meet her here,' Eve assured him.

'Can we go on the lake?' he asked, wriggling on the chair, which was too low for him.

'I expect so. I think you ought to have a sleep after lunch.'

For Eve the day passed slowly, but by

nightfall she was beginning to feel the effects of her sleepless night on the train. She went to bed early and awoke the next morning feeling more refreshed than she had been for some days. It's the mountain air, she told herself as she stood on the balcony of their room and gazed at the wooded hills with their shady pine trees.

She was in the writing-room scribbling a few lines to Anita, informing her where she and Tommy were staying, when a maid came in and told her that there was a lady waiting to see her in the lounge. Eve's excitement mounted as she took Tommy's hand and followed the girl into the room which faced a sweep of vivid green grass.

'Nadia!' Eve exclaimed as she walked quickly across to the doctor, who was looking exceptionally attractive in a white dress and scarlet jacket. 'I've been so worried about you! When did you get here?'

Nadia kissed her, then bent down to hug Tommy. 'I arrived two days ago, but they were booked up here. I've checked in at another hotel.' She straightened, but retained Tommy's small hand. 'I didn't think you would come so soon, otherwise I would have called in before.'

'We arrived yesterday. The reception clerk told us that there had been a cancellation, so we were lucky. Samira was becoming suspicious about your illness. Dean wanted to get us away before she found out that you had gone.'

'My illness?' Nadia laughed. 'Is that what you told her?'

'Yes. Samira thought you had something infectious, so it was easy to keep her from going to the den.'

'Yes, she would be frightened. That was clever of you.'

'Dean said he would leave as soon as he could.'

Nadia nodded absent-mindedly. She was gazing out of the french windows, intent on the figure of a man who had his back turned towards them. He was wearing white slacks and a dark blue shirt and the sun glinted on his fair hair.

'I want you to come and meet someone,' Nadia said with a faint smile. 'We can go out this way. Don't be afraid, Tommy.' Pulling the boy to the windows, she pushed one open and stepped out on to the grass.

Eve followed them, then halted, almost overcome with relief and astonishment. Dean! How had he got here so quickly? For a second or two she was unable to move, then, conscious of quickening heart beats, she moved towards the man.

The tall figure swung round and Eve stared at him, her eyes widening with astonishment. Then a sickening sense of disappointment swamped her as she realised it was not Dean, but someone very like him. Blue eyes in a brown face resembling Dean's were twinkling down at her.

Nadia took her hand. 'I'm sorry, Eve, to give you such a shock. We hated having to deceive you. But now you can meet the real Dean. This is the man I'm going to marry.'

The man smiled. 'Nadia's told me how helpful you've been, Eve. I can't thank you enough. There's so much I want to say, but I guess you will understand that I have to greet my son first.'

Eve glanced at Tommy doubtfully. It was almost too much to expect a boy of his age to accept this change of roles.

Dean was stretching out his hands. 'Hi, junior! Haven't you got a kiss for your pa? You didn't expect to see me, I bet.'

Tommy hung back, scowling. 'You're not my Daddy,' he said truculently.

'I know how you feel, son. It's bewildering, isn't it? Come and see something!' Dean thrust his hand in his trouser pocket and pulled out a snapshot. 'Hi! Don't you want to see it?'

Tommy advanced cautiously and stared at the picture. 'That's me!' he cried.

'Yes, and who is that next to you and Aunt Anita?'

Tommy looked up at him and blinked. 'You are my Daddy?'

'I sure am. Your real one.' Dean smiled and picked him up. 'Want a ride on my shoulders? I bet Uncle Pete never did that.'

Tommy shook his head, too dumbfounded to speak, but he made no protest at taking a ride on his father's back. Eve was staring at them with a dazed expression on her face. Nadia glanced at her and put her arm around her waist in sympathy.

'I do apologise, Eve. It wasn't a nice trick to play on you. The man you thought was Dean is his twin brother, Pete. They look so alike. Only when you really know them do you see differences.'

Eve nodded. 'This Dean is browner. When he had his back turned I thought it was Dean . . . Pete,' she added in confusion.

'It will take time to get used to it,'

Nadia said with understanding. 'It was important that Dean had someone to take his place when he had to go off on an assignment. Dean works for American Intelligence.'

Eve released a deep sigh. 'I'm beginning to understand. But I'm worried about Tommy. He's had to manage without parents for so long and within the last three months has had two daddies. The poor boy must be so confused.'

Nadia nodded her head. 'Yes. It was selfish of me to have him sent across to Morocco. Dean and I didn't stop to think how it might trouble Tommy. Having waited so long to get married, our one thought was to settle down in Tangier with the boy. Dean thought we ought to get acquainted before the wedding, so that's why he asked Pete to write to Anita.'

'Do Dean and Pete write alike also?'

Nadia laughed. 'I don't think so. Dean signed his name at the bottom of a blank sheet of paper. Pete typed the contents.'

'So that accounts for the long letter. Anita said Dean never wrote more than a few lines.'

'Yes, he's more careless than his brother. His mind is so occupied with his career that he tends to be rather selfish about other people.' She smiled. 'You see, although I love him dearly I haven't closed my eyes to his faults. He has a 'devil may care' attitude to life, due no doubt to his hazardous way of living. He's been in constant danger ever since I've known him.'

Eve glanced at the man who had moved away to play with Tommy and noticed that he was coming back to Nadia. 'I can see now that Tommy's version of his father was correct. The boy has noticed it, too. Pete was very sensible. He never took much notice of Tommy. I thought it very strange, but I can see why he didn't want the boy to become too fond of him.'

'Yes. Pete didn't agree about having Tommy with him, but as it turned out I think he was pleased because he met you.'

Eve frowned and looked at Dean. 'Do you think your brother will be able to get out safely?'

Dean's eyes narrowed and his face tightened. 'That I can't promise. But if he doesn't turn up within a couple of days I shall fly across to Tangier.'

Eve swallowed painfully. 'I expect Nadia has told you that he has been watched all the time?'

'Sure. We expected that. In fact we wanted that to happen. He was to be the sitting pigeon.'

'I do wish I had known!' Eve exclaimed in distress.

'You couldn't have altered anything. In fact, if you had known it would have made it more awkward for Pete. Naturally if I had guessed that Nadia was going to be suspected I would not have asked for Tommy to be sent out.'

'You intended to go back there?'

'Yes. My cover was good. Pete was seeing to that. I planned to marry

Nadia and live in Tangier.'

'What will you do now?'

Dean looked at Nadia and smiled. 'I've been recalled. I'm no longer considered a good risk in Europe and North Africa. I've been offered a post in America. Nadia is pleased and it will be better for Tommy.'

'Does your brother live in America?'

'San Francisco. He's a history professor and lecturer.'

Eve nodded. That did fit in. No wonder Pete had been so keen on discussing the history of Morocco. She did not ask any more questions for she was beginning to fit the pieces together herself and was dazed at the process. Also she was consumed with fear that Pete might not be as fortunate as his brother. Thinking that in her present state she would not be good company for the newly united couple, she pleaded a headache and spent the rest of the morning in her room.

Nadia took Tommy back to the hotel half an hour before dinner. 'Dean and I think he ought to stay with you until Pete arrives,' she explained. 'He will take your mind off this worrying, waiting business. When he does come we will take Tommy and you will be free to do as you wish.'

Eve had risen from her chair close to the balcony of her room when Nadia came in with Tommy and her face was hidden from the light. But when she moved the doctor could see something was wrong.

'My dear, you don't look well,' she exclaimed compassionately. 'Are you worrying about Pete?'

Eve nodded, giving her a faint smile. 'Silly, isn't it? I can't do anything. My legs feel like jelly. It's not knowing what is happening.'

'I know. I've had months of it. That's why I'm so thankful we are going back to America. I can't give you much comfort, I guess, but Pete knows how to look after himself. Considering it's not his line of country, he's done extraordinarily well.'

'He said he was no good at play acting.' Eve smiled. 'At the time I didn't understand. Now I know what he meant.'

Nadia stared at her thoughtfully. 'I'm so glad that you feel like that about Pete. I often wondered. It couldn't have been easy for you when I arrived. You hid your feelings so well.'

Eve said quietly, 'I didn't want to embarrass you and I thought Dean . . . I mean Pete . . . was in love with you.'

'Would you like me to wait until Tommy is asleep?' Nadia asked. 'We could go back to my hotel for dinner. You won't feel so alone there.'

'No.' Eve smiled. 'It's good of you, Nadia, but I would be dull company. I shall go to bed early.'

'Okay then. I will see you in the morning. Dean is taking us across the lake. He knows someone with a motor boat.'

'Tommy will like that.'

'Yes. He's accepted Dean very

quickly. That makes me feel less guilty, I guess.'

'He's a good child and he's very fond of you, Nadia.'

'I'm real lucky. I never expected it to be so easy. Yet at the same time I feel afraid.'

'I can understand that,' Eve said seriously. 'I'm scared to hope for anything.'

Nadia chuckled. 'That's only because you are so keyed up. Your problems will solve themselves. I shall have to go. Dean is waiting for me and I've made you late for dinner.'

Eve gave Tommy his bath, settled him down for the night, then waited until he had dropped off to sleep. She did not hurry as she changed into a green and white dress chosen at random. It was one she had bought in Paris, and if her mind had been on what she was doing she would not have put it on. She had planned to wear it when a special occasion cropped up. However, it did help to cheer her up a little when she noticed that it suited her so well.

When she entered the dining-room she found that the meal was half over, so she skipped the soup and fish courses. Luckily she did not feel hungry. She had a table to herself and felt very lonely and remote as she listened to the conversation of the other guests.

She was crossing the entrance hall on her way to her room when she heard her name called. The voice was so familiar that her heart leapt for joy. But when she twisted round to see whom it was her disappointment brought stinging tears to her eyes. There was a man there, a seaman, and he was standing in front of the door gazing at her. He wore a navy blue jersey, black trousers, and had a shiny peaked cap on his head. His face was dirty and unshaven. She could not see his eyes for he was standing away from the light. Yet there was something in the way he was standing which fascinated her and she remained still looking at him intently. Then feeling slightly foolish, she began to turn away.

'Eve! Don't go.'

When she turned back she saw that he had removed his cap. One look at that crop of fair hair and she forgot all caution. Overjoyed, she rushed across to him.

'Dean!' she exclaimed, all her fears miraculously disappearing as she flung herself into his arms. 'You're safe. Thank God, you are safe!' Tears streamed down her cheeks as she held on to him tightly.

Pete kissed her hard on the lips. 'Sure, honey. I told you I would come.'

The guests were beginning to drift from the dining-room and, conscious of their curious eyes, Pete said urgently, 'Let's get out of here. I've so much to say to you.'

'I called you Dean,' she said shakily. 'I'm not used to your real name yet.'

'Never mind, honey. Anything sounds good to me,' he muttered as he drew her towards the entrance and opened the door.

'When did you arrive?' Eve asked breathlessly as he walked her swiftly away from the hotel towards the lake.

'Only a few minutes ago. I didn't wait to clean up. I had to see you.'

Eve was beginning to feel a little foolish. She had greeted him so enthusiastically, without a thought about his feelings. 'I'm sorry. I got carried away,' she said with a light laugh. 'I've been so anxious about you. Then seeing you suddenly like that, it was too much.'

'Don't apologise, I liked it.' Pete stopped and put his arm about her waist. 'I've been in love with you from the moment I first saw you. So many times I tried to tell you how I felt. But it was impossible with Nadia there. I guess she has explained to you.' He gave her a searching look. 'She is here, isn't she?'

Eve laughed shakily. 'Yes and your brother is with her.'

Pete sighed. 'That's the best news

I've heard in a long time. Are they staying at the Mignon?'

'No. They couldn't get in. But they aren't far away. I can take you to their hotel. Dean has met Tommy.'

'How much have they told you?'

'Most of it, I think. I know who you are and now I understand why you were so interested in old Morocco.'

Pete laughed ruefully. 'That was one of the candies I had dangled in front of me. I guess I wasn't too keen when Dean's boss suggested I come over and take his place. I had never done anything more dangerous than hunting moose and shooting jack rabbits. These last three months have been a nightmare.'

'How did you manage to swop places with your brother?'

'We did it here in the Hotel Mignon. Dean handed over all his possessions right down to his clothes; everything except his shoes, which were too large for me. Then I flew to Tangier and took up residence in his house. Dean wasn't being watched at that time. His enemies hadn't started to become suspicious so his flight to Switzerland had not been observed. Everything was new to me. I had to find out where his office was and I had to keep myself out of sight as much as possible. I had been told that on no account was I to leave Tangier or go to the Country Club. But I did have to show myself so that his enemies would know he was around.'

'What did you do in the office all day?'

Pete grinned and gave her a quick hug. 'I played chess, read, cleared up Dean's paperwork and generally tried to give the impression that everything was progressing as usual. I did manage to make a few friends of my own. They helped. If it hadn't been for Ali-ben-Ahmed I couldn't have survived. He guessed that I was someone other than I appeared to be, although he never said so. But I gathered from his conversation and the hints he dropped that he was a staunch supporter of law and order. He brought or sent merchants to see me, pretending that they had business for me. It made it look more authentic.'

'Nadia told me that you wrote that letter to Anita.'

'Yes. Dean asked me to write to her before I left Switzerland. I posted it in Tangier much against my will. I didn't approve of having Tommy there with me. I thought it was too dangerous. Also it was unfair on the boy. Then, when you turned up with Tommy, my scruples vanished. For a time at least. I soon found there were to be other problems. Tommy was supposed to stay with me until Nadia arrived. Then when his mission was accomplished Dean would join us. I was to keep out of sight until I could be smuggled out of the country. Nadia and Dean were going to stay in Tangier with Tommy.'

'The attacks on Nadia's life altered that,' Eve said.

'It sure did. Dean had told me that he needed at least three months. He didn't think it would take that long, but that was the time limit. That's why when Nadia left I had to stay on. I was terribly worried about you, Eve, and being in love with you didn't help. You see, I wasn't sure whether you and Evan were serious about one another. I felt mean asking you to leave. But by then you were too involved. I had to think of your safety.'

'I was never in love with Evan,' Eve said seriously.

Pete drew her swiftly into the dark shadows of an ancient tree and enfolded her in his arms. 'Darling . . . I love you so much. I guess I never did believe you were keen on Evan. But that didn't stop me being jealous. And I was afraid that when you found out that I had been deceiving you I wouldn't stand a chance.'

Eve chuckled. 'You would have to do something really terrible to make me fall out of love. I'm afraid I'm incurable. I think I knew that when you kissed me that first time on the roof.'

'Yes. I would not have dared to do

that so soon after meeting you. But I was real scared when you nearly fell and it seemed the natural thing to do. Afterwards I was glad because I realised you didn't find me objectionable.'

She laughed. 'Far from it. I was ashamed of myself. Yet it did prove that I was in danger of falling in love with you. Not that I heeded that warning, for when Nadia arrived I was too deeply in love to do much about it.'

'If only I could have told you about Nadia,' he said contritely as he pulled her closer and kissed her forehead.

Unresistingly she raised her face so that he could find her lips, her heart beating in unison with his as he showed his need for her. Past, present and future faded into insignificance as she strained to him, accepting and forgiving the fierceness of his caresses.

'Honey . . . ' he muttered hoarsely, 'I have to know how you feel about spending the rest of your life with me. You are going to marry me? I'm in no mood for refusals.'

She said shakily, 'I'm so frightened I shall wake up and find it's all a dream.'

'It's no dream, honey. I'm here and waiting for an answer.'

'How idiotic! You know what it is . . . yes, yes, yes!'

He sighed then kissed her gently. 'Until you ran to me in the hotel lobby I was gravely in doubt. There had been times when I hoped, but you covered your feelings so adroitly. You even had me thinking that it was Evan you cared for.'

'That was deliberate, I'm afraid. I thought you were going to marry Nadia. I had to pretend I didn't care.'

'I'm real sorry I had to deceive you so much. I was living on a tight rope all the time and one slip could have meant disaster.'

'No wonder you ran away when Gloria called! By the way, how did you know it was her?'

Pete chuckled. 'Dean had warned me about her and he had given me a detailed description. He told me about

Tangier and what to expect and briefly described the people he knew. The trouble was that my brother was so well known and popular. I had to become a recluse, showing myself but never coming in close contact with the folk he knew well. Gloria and Dean had quite a thing going for them some time ago. That was before he met Nadia. He told me that the woman was persistent. I knew that if she ever came face to face with me the fat would be in the fire. She talks too much and it would soon have got around that I was not Dean.'

'Did your brother tell you why he had to leave Tangier?'

'Are you kidding, honey?' Pete laughed. 'Dean never mentions his work. His boss told me that Dean had stumbled on some important information and that it was vital that no one should know that he had heard of it or passed it on. When I met Dean in Switzerland he did explain that it was Nadia who had been his informant. But he only told me that because he was worried about her safety. He had known her a couple of years and during that time she had given him many useful bits of news she had picked up in the nomad camps. And the last time she met Dean in Fez she gave him something so important that he had to act on it immediately. Apparently some plot was afoot to overthrow the government. The instigators were getting an army together on the borders of Algeria. I doubt whether they would have been successful, but many innocent people would have been killed. I imagine that Algeria is where Dean went, but it is pointless to ask him. As nothing has happened I assume he's nipped it in the bud. A word in the right ears can work wonders. So much happens behind the scenes that the average citizen knows nothing about.'

Eve nodded her head. 'Ali-ben-Ahmed believed something was happening, otherwise he wouldn't have helped you.'

'I guess so. Ali thought I knew more

than I did, for he expressed his gratitude on more than one occasion.'

'If Nadia hadn't been suspected, then Dean's cover would still be safe.'

'That's right. Dean told me he had a fifty-fifty chance of getting away with it. He warned me that I might be watched. His association with Nadia would have been noticed, but if Nadia hadn't been found out he would have been in the clear. I imagine he's been able to do some valuable work under cover of his phoney business. That, I'm afraid, has ended.'

They left their shady retreat and strolled on towards the lake, arms entwined. Above them in a velvety dark sky the full moon sailed majestically, shedding a mellow light over the scene about them.

Unheedingly Eve asked curiously, 'How did you get on after I left?'

'I don't know what happened to Samira. I didn't go back to the house again. I stayed with Ali's family until he could arrange for me to leave on one of his cargo boats.' He grinned. 'That's why I look like this. I've been working my passage up the coast of Spain and Portugal. When I reached France I disembarked and travelled overland to Paris. Then I flew to Geneva and here I am.'

'I expect you feel exhausted,' Eve exclaimed. 'How dreadful of me not to have thought of it before! Are you hungry? Shall we go back to the hotel?'

'Not yet. I had a meal before I left Geneva. What I do need is a bath, shave and a change of clothes. I've left all my possessions, or rather, Dean's personal things, behind me. All I have is what I'm wearing.'

'Did you leave your clothes at the Mignon?'

'I'm hoping they are there. Dean said he would arrange for them to be looked after.' He paused to glance at her. 'Something bothering you, honey? You seem pensive.'

She smiled. 'Not really. I was thinking of that morning on the beach when you met Evan. Was that really the first time you had seen him?'

'Yes. As a matter of fact he gave me a terrific jolt when he said he had met me. If he hadn't mentioned Gloria's name I wouldn't have had any idea of his identity.'

'You covered up very well. I noticed nothing. I'm surprised that Evan took you for Dean.'

'Dean didn't know him. Evan only came to Tangier four months before I did. My brother included him in the list of acquaintances, but said that there was no need to bother about him. I bet Dean forgot about that cocktail party. I must confess I felt real uneasy whenever he was around.'

'You needn't have worried. Evan obviously thought you were Dean. You look so alike. You would have to stand side by side for an acquaintance to detect any difference.'

'Sure. It's helped to get us out of a few scrapes when we were younger.' He smiled ruefully. 'I didn't bargain on having to continue the treatment.'

'I expect Nadia is upset. She's lost all her clothes and you had to leave your books behind!'

'Nadia will enjoy buying new ones. As for the books, most of them belong to Dean. His expenses will pay for our losses. Later I shall have to go and see him, but before I do that I want to have everything settled between us.' He gave her an enquiring look. 'Do you have to go back to England?'

Eve shook her head. 'There's no one to go back for. My parents are dead. There's only my sister. I shall regret not seeing her, but she will understand and will send my things to me. I can write to the school and Anita. There's really no point in going back.'

'That's wonderful. We can stay here for a week or two if you wish. I would prefer to marry in San Francisco. My parents live there. They will want to hear about Dean, Tommy and Nadia.'

Eve smiled. 'They will be able to tell them themselves. Dean is being sent back to America.'

'Is that a fact? That's real good news. In that case we can all fly back together.' He put his arm about Eve's waist and swung her into the air. 'Gosh, I haven't felt so happy in a long time!'

'It's going to take me some time to get used to calling you Pete,' Eve said breathlessly as he set her down.

'I reckon that won't bother me much as long as you stay with me,' he exclaimed, smiling lovingly at her serious profile. Then as he drew her closer his smile broadened into a grin. 'There is one reservation,' he stated firmly.

'Oh, what's that?' she asked innocently.

'Never, ever, call me Mr Rimmer!' His blue eyes twinkled. 'Every time you referred to me by my surname it was like a douche of icy cold water. I lost ground every time you said it.' He laughed. 'It's amazing, now I come to think of it!'

Eve's green eyes sparkled, but she

kept her voice grave. 'If it's going to restore your confidence I promise never to do it again.'

'That's sweet of you, honey, but I guess it's asking too much. Now stop teasing and give me a kiss. It's time we went in search of Dean and Nadia.'

Bemused and bewitched, Eve ran into his arms and for a few minutes escaped into a wordless world that was rich with promise of their future together.

THE END